The Man from Next Door

The Man from Next Door

a novel by

HONOR TRACY

Random House
New York

Library of Congress Cataloging in Publication Data
Tracy, Honor Lilbush Wingfield, 1915-
The man from next door.
I. Title.
PZ4.T762Man3   [PR6070.R25]   823'.9'14   76-53473
ISBN 0-394-40279-0

Manufactured in the United States of America
24689753
First American Edition

To
Bill Gingerich

The tale as told by
Penelope Butler

Foreword

I am going to put my story down in black and white, just as it happened, hoping once it is finished to find even one little thread of sense in it, one little pointer as to why Cruise should have acted as he did. Up to the present, turning it over and over in my poor weary brain, I have found nothing at all. Indeed, the more I ponder, the more utterly baffling does it become. But if, rather than grope for reasons, I simply chronicle the events and then consider them as calmly and dispassionately as I can, it may be that light will somehow dawn.

The account shall be as full as possible, because in a case so entirely mysterious there is no telling what may be relevant to it. Cruise's wicked treatment of me was puzzling enough, as I had done him no manner of harm; but why, not content with that, he should have coldbloodedly set to work to bring about my ruin as if I, not he, were the offender, is beyond all comprehension. Plainly, he had some terrible grudge against me; but, what in heaven's name was the cause?

Well, I have paper and pen and ample leisure to arrange my thoughts. On remand there is plenty of time to spare and, as you are not yet convicted, you may occupy it much as you please. The date of the trial is not even fixed, as the police are still busy with their inquiries. There are weeks, perhaps months, ahead of me for meditation and analysis. Of the final outcome I have no fears. Wholly innocent, I put my faith in God and English justice. The important thing for me now is to try and fathom the mind of Cruise; for unless I can, I really believe that my own mind will be in danger of overthrow. I do indeed.

Penelope Butler

One

Cruise came into my life by knocking at my door and asking if I had seen his cat. It sounds a simple matter but, in fact, such conduct was most unusual in Norfolk House. The tenants of the various flats into which the building was divided held no communication with each other, beyond a formal greeting if they met upon the stairs. It was an unwritten law, observed by everyone. You knew the various different names because you saw them on letters collected in a communal basket in the hall, and you could guess which belonged to which vaguely familiar figure; but to have shown any interest, by—for instance—asking Bert the caretaker, who took the rubbish away and swept the stairs, would have been a breach of etiquette. And if, coming for your letters, you found someone else there, you stood a little way off until he had finished. To have hovered round him might have seemed like an attack on his privacy.

The house itself stood in a pleasant London square, with a garden of trees and flowers in the centre. It formed one end to this garden, and an equally large house formed the end opposite, while the two sides had iron railings and a gate for the use of the other square-dwellers. They of course had to let themselves in with a key, whereas we could walk straight in, and this gave us the feeling that we were special and that people with keys really had no business in the garden at all. It was a quiet little spot except when the dustmen came round, banging and howling; but they were so often on strike that there were long periods of unbroken peace. It was also a little enclave of Englishness, with tweedy low-voiced women, polite bowler-hatted men, nicely mannered children and cared-for dogs, a contrast to the area round it which swarmed with Negroes, Arabs, Indians and a whole European tutti frutti, jabbering and gesticulating, throwing litter about and generally making themselves at home.

In Norfolk House, every single tenant had an English name, which was unusual for the Royal Borough of Kensington. All the correspondence in the basket had educated writing on it or came from establishments of repute, and appeared to be addressed to the same kind of people. That was interesting too, because of the way in which the rooms were split up. The mezzanine and the *bel étage* were both a single, very expensive, flat, while the floors above them were divided in two, costing less the higher they stood. This discrepancy in the rent should have led to different types of person taking the accommodation, but such was evidently not the case. Indeed, the atmosphere of the place was rather that of a good old-fashioned club, with everyone politely going his own way, minding his own business and avoiding anything so unseemly as a casual encounter or scraped acquaintance.

I had one of the two smaller flats at the very top of the house. Even that would have been far beyond my resources but for a sudden amazing piece of fortune that came my way a year ago, which I will speak of presently. Besides the kitchen, bath and hall, there were three good rooms with the big sash windows and the high ceilings of their epoch, so unlike the cramped box of a dwelling which I had left. Looking out of the windows in front, I was on a level with the treetops of the garden and from the rear, there was a splendid view over the roofs and towers of London.

From the first day I moved in, I felt at home in these surroundings and in tune with the orderly, reserved spirit of the establishment. So much so that, as often happens when circumstances improve, I wondered how I could have put up with things as they were before: the paper-thin walls of that block, the noise of children, telephones, transistors, footsteps overhead

6

or on the uncarpeted stairs, the smells of cooking and un-collected rubbish, the lift out of order for days on end and the camaraderie of my fellow tenants. Here, my life was one long round of quiet pleasure. It may be thought that a young woman of ample means should have occupied herself in social or welfare work; but I had had too much experience both of the recipients of State charity and those who dispensed it ever to do that. The latter, especially, put me off : it seems to be a law of nature that people who have messed up their own lives should feel an urge to guide and control the lives of others. Divorcees, misfits, failures, how well I knew them, and how sorry I always felt for their helpless charges! So, for the present anyhow, I was taking things easily, revelling in my new situation, going to art exhibitions, concerts, theatres, enter-taining my friends in the manner I had always aspired to, buying the books and gramophone records that interested me, enjoying all for which, previously, there had never been money or time. I watched the world setting off for the daily grind without a pang, indeed, if anything with added appreciation of my own good luck, as someone lying safe and snug in a warm bed harkens contentedly to the wind and rain outside. It may sound selfish and probably was, but I had been through the mill and daily thanked my stars I was out of it.

And then, one evening, there came a brisk, somewhat per-emptory, tattoo on my knocker; and, opening the door, I found myself face to face with a broadly smiling young man in shirt-sleeves, who inquired : 'Have you by any chance seen my cat?'

*

Taken by surprise, I asked him what it was like, which was foolish of me because I had not seen, or noticed, any cats at all.

'A beautiful marmalade,' he said. 'Big and strong, a sort of mini tiger, with eyes like two green shining marbles. He is more of a brother than a pet. Answers to the name of Duke.'

7

'I have not come across any cat of that description, I am afraid.'

'We have only just arrived,' the visitor said. 'I am the man from next door.' He made the disclosure with peculiar emphasis, plainly thinking it of importance to me. 'My name is Cruise, Johnny to friends.'

Over the past few days I had seen this name on letters and parcels and had been vaguely conscious of someone moving into the flat beside mine.

'It must be, he felt strange in the new surroundings and took himself off,' the visitor continued. 'It is terrible to imagine him shut in somewhere, or run over. Or stolen, perhaps for vivisection.' It might have been a lonely old woman talking, and yet the voice was oddly unconcerned. 'What do you say to vivisection, Miss Butler?'

The use of my name and the request for a personal opinion struck me as rather forward, and in any case I was busy cooking my supper. 'I haven't really thought about it,' I replied. 'Will you excuse me?' And I made as if to shut the door.

Mr Cruise was nothing daunted. 'I call it a blot on humanity,' he said. And now, with the greatest calm in the world, he slipped in past me and began to study one of the pictures on the wall. 'That's a Paul Henrey, isn't it?'

'No.' I should have left it there, but something made me add: 'A Paul Klee.'

'Well, I got part of it right anyhow,' he said with cheerful triumph. 'Is it genu-ine?' That pronunciation, and a certain lilt in his voice should have warned me, for I had heard them often enough; but I was too concerned for my Wiener Schnitzel to think about anything else.

'As far as I know. Now, if you will kindly excuse me . . .'

But I might have been talking to empty air, in fact was doing so, for with quick light steps he had scampered through the hall and into the sitting-room. I followed in rising indignation and found him looking it over with an air of appraisal.

'Charming,' he said. 'How well you have done it all up. One can see that you have very good taste.'

With that, he sank into one of my easy chairs and comfortably crossed his legs. It occurred to me that he was possibly mad, and yet he did not look it, not at least as I should have expected a madman to look; but who can tell in this troubled era. If conduct was anything to go by, he could hardly muster as normal, but there was nothing disturbed in his manner. On the contrary, it was relaxed and assured, and he spoke as if from the start I had made him entirely welcome. That imperviousness to rebuff was oddly disconcerting, moreover: I could not think for the moment what to say next, and stood helplessly by while he smiled up at me in the friendliest way imaginable.

He was in his mid or late twenties, or so I judged, roughly the same age as myself, not bad-looking in an obvious kind of way, with brown curly hair and large hazel eyes flecked with green. And—another point in his favour—he was clean-shaven. His trousers were of a dark grey cloth, not the eternal grubby blue denim, and his shirt was good. But where was his jacket? It was one thing to knock at my door in his shirt-sleeves, inquiring for a cat, but quite another to pay a call in this garb; and to pay a call was clearly what he had in mind.

'A penny for your thoughts,' he said cosily, fanning my irritation. My Christian name is Penelope, and the stress he laid on 'penny' showed that he knew it, even that, unless I could tame him, he would shortly be using it.

'I was wondering, frankly, to what I owe this visit.'

'I'm your neighbour! Isn't that reason enough? Don't be starchy. I can't believe you are starchy deep down,' he said, with a familiarity that made me grind my teeth. 'And—I may as well be honest with you—I could fancy a drink. I'm out of it myself.'

'Then perhaps you had better go to a public-house. There are plenty of them round here.'

For the first time a spark of resentment showed in his eye.

9

'What a thing to say!' he cried. 'Look at those bottles over there! Enough to open a public-house yourself.'

'But I have no idea of opening a public-house,' I retorted, losing patience. 'Now, please, will you go? There are a number of things I have to do.'

His next words fairly took my breath away.

'But why should you, just you, be so stand-offish, when everyone else in the house is so free and easy?'

'Free and easy?' I echoed, in amazement. 'They are nothing of the sort. That is what I like about them. They don't come dropping in on one. They keep themselves to themselves.'

'They may do, with you,' he returned calmly. 'But that is because, if you don't mind my saying so, you are considered a dark horse.'

I began to think I was dreaming.

'A dark horse? How can I possibly be a dark horse? Who has said so?' I demanded angrily.

'It seems to be the general opinion. I don't care. Your life is your own. But I thought you might be lonely sometimes, and I wanted to cheer you up.'

Would that I had shown him to the door without further discussion! But things had gone too far: I could not leave them at that. 'I insist on your telling me exactly what you mean,' I hammered on.

'I don't mean anything. I know nothing about it. But you move in here, into an expensive flat, from somewhere in Camden Town, as your forwarded letters show, without an occupation or visible means of support. People don't know what to make of it. But it's no business of theirs or mine.' He treated me to a man-of-the-worldly smile. 'I merely say, they are forthcoming enough as a rule. Yes, very forthcoming,' he repeated, and again looked wistfully at the bottles of drink on their tray.

Here, incidentally, I should explain that he had received an entirely false impression from the number of bottles standing there. Except at a meal, I only drink sherry, and that now and then, and the vodka, whisky, Pernod, Bacardi, gin, were for my friends, all of whom had their own preferences and kept to them. It was clear that he imagined tippling to be one of my dubious practices, whatever these were, but I was too confounded by his revelations to try and correct him. All I wanted was that he should go and allow me to arrange my troubled thoughts in peace.

'If I see your cat I will tell the caretaker,' I said. 'And now . . .'

Reluctantly, he took his eyes off the bottles and turned them on me with an air of inquiry. 'Cat?' he asked : then, quickly, 'Ah yes, to be sure. Yes, do that. Poor old Marmaduke!' I realised, there was no cat. The impudence of the fellow was past believing. 'Well, I don't think you are in the mood for company tonight,' he went on, as if this possibility had only just occurred to him. Slowly he got to his feet. 'But you know where to find me now. If there is anything I can do for you any time, don't hesitate to ask.'

And with a last flashing smile he went away.

*

In the space of a few minutes he had turned everything upside down. The pleasant house where I lived and everyone in it took on an entirely new and evil aspect. Far from going their own way and minding their own business, my fellow tenants pored over a newcomer's correspondence and made deductions from it. What I had taken for well-bred reserve was the holding at arm's length of one who was probably undesirable. There was no doubt in my mind but that Cruise had spoken the truth. Certainly, he had invented the cat as a pretext for starting a conversation, but he could not have known, by himself, of my previous humble address. Months had passed since anything was forwarded on from there, and he had only been in the house a few days. Someone had told him of it, and talked of me freely, suspiciously, disparagingly.

And cruelly, and unjustly. Why on earth, because I had moved to better surroundings, should I be a dark horse? And what did my having no occupation signify? And where did 'no visible means of support' come in, when I regularly paid the rent and had furnished the place in lavish style to my liking? What if I had inherited money? Who was to say that I hadn't? Merely by coming to wealth, of course, one cannot immediately acquire the ways of moneyed people. No doubt, in my appearance, speech, deportment, I was still the ordinary working woman that I always had been. But why this should give rise to odious speculations was past comprehending.

There was the question too, of what precise form my detrimental proclivities were supposed to take. The tenants could hardly imagine I might be a call girl, for there were no male visitors racketing up and down the stairs. Nor that I was running a joint in Soho, since often as not I stayed quietly at home. This habit further ruled out the chance of my being a Russian spy, or a bank robber, or a drug pusher, all of which would call for mobility and organisation. Unless I were living by blackmail, then, there seemed no criminal or immoral pursuit that was open to one of my circumstances.

Such were the notions that raced through my head as I sat there this sunny evening in June, with the scent of lime-flowers wafting in from the garden and the cooing of doves in my ears: two things I loved, from which all pleasure now was gone. They were wild and lurid fancies, of course, quite disproportionate to the few guarded hints that Cruise had dropped. But for one of relatively blameless life to hear, all at once, that she is reckoned a dark horse does not conduce to rational thought. I felt shaken and miserable, and in some curious way guilty, though of what I could not have said.

But I must not ramble on in this manner, or get carried away on side issues. Now I will reveal the secret of my sudden affluence, something so trite, even vulgar, that I had carefully kept it dark; and I will tell enough of my history before wealth came my way to explain how completely off-course I was blown.

I won a large, indeed an enormous, sum on the Football Pools. How this came about is a puzzle, for I understand nothing of football and take no interest in it. Had I filled in the form blindfold, my entries could scarcely have been more haphazard. A friend of mine had won a few hundreds in this way and, tired of pinching and scraping, I determined to try it as well. It was as if an angel guided my pen, while other angels drove all other pens astray, for after half a dozen attempts this mammoth booty was mine.

I suppose the mind is unable to take in events of such magnitude all at once. Often and often I had indulged in daydreams of what I should do, if ever I got the money. Now it was there, my reaction was one of simple acute embarrassment. I remembered reading of similar cases in the Press, with pictures of men or women waving their cheques at the camera while they babbled of Rolls Royces, mink coats or villas in Spain, and the first decision I took was to avoid anything of the kind myself. Apart from the public shame, there was the fear of being kidnapped for ransom, an almost daily occurrence at the time. The promoters were naturally disappointed, but I was firm; and from that day to this only they, and my Bank, knew what had happened.

As anyone familiar with the Lord Chesterfield Comprehensive School will understand, my next and immediate step was to resign from it. I had been teaching art there, or rather, was paid to do so. It is impossible to teach what nobody wants to learn, either because he thinks he knows enough already or because the subject has no appeal for him. To a child, the pupils were convinced that learning to draw was a waste of time, and the headmaster backed them to the hilt. My duty, he always said, was to help them 'feel their way to a valid self-expression', and I was not even allowed to criticise the horrible fruits of this. One thing I will say : they were too busy daubing and smearing to offer me violence. Pitched battles were frequent in most other classes. The mathematics master was carried to hospital the day I resigned, and a week before that the chemistry mistress lost her eyebrows through an explosion, a bomb having been fitted under the lid of her desk.

The Head received the news of my intention with grieved surprise.

'But why should you go? Have you another job in view?' he asked. 'Where will you find any work as rewarding as ours?'

'This is why,' and I passed him the crude depiction of a naked man, the genitals twice as big as the rest of the body and painted a vivid cobalt. There was a caption to it, *Studdy in Blu*, and a signature, Siva Rampat. 'I can bear no more.' And I thought with a pang of life-classes at the Ruskin, Oxford, and of all I had hoped to achieve in those days.

'I can't see much wrong with that,' said the Head, examining the work with close attention. 'It strikes me as an unusual theme and a vigorous treatment.'

'Hardly unusual, Headmaster. This boy never draws anything else.'

'But you know, Miss Butler, in a multi-racial school like ours, we must allow for and accommodate cultural strains that will often seem at variance with our own. Much of the best Indian art was always, to our way of thinking, obscene. Siva is following in an old tradition, whatever you and I may feel about it. Our aim, surely, must be to help him develop along that traditional line.'

'Well, I don't consider myself the person to do it,' I told him.

'There I disagree. I have always looked on you as one of our most successful teachers here,' he said kindly. 'When it comes to pupil-involvement, your record is unsurpassed. There has not been so much as a window broken since you came. In your predecessor's time, as often as not, the studio was a total wreck.'

This was all most gratifying, but I could not be persuaded. When he saw that my mind was made up, like the decent

14

fellow he was, he consented to my leaving at break-up, then but a few days off, without requiring the usual full term's notice. And so, very soon, I walked out of the place for ever, as free as a bird and my heart singing inside me.

Now came the task of beginning a new kind of life, which to me only meant reverting to a former one. In the day dreams I spoke of, there had been nothing extravagant or exotic, no buying my way into worlds where I did not belong. All I wanted was to live as I had done, and among the same sort of people, up to the age of twelve, when my parents were both carried off by Asian flu within a week of each other. My father was the leading solicitor of Norwich and I, an only child, was brought up in comfort, with ponies to ride, holidays abroad with my parents, toys, books, nice clothes and good food, pretty objects round me, and any reasonable wish I had granted at once. But this same man who so brilliantly managed the affairs of half of Norfolk had left his own in indescribable confusion. When at last everything was sorted out and his innumerable debts were paid, what all had assumed to be a substantial fortune was revealed as a mere nest egg.

I have no complaint whatever of the aunt who unhesitatingly took charge of me. She made no difference between me and her own children, and she handed my father's modest legacy to me intact on my coming of age, enabling me to go to the Ruskin College of Art. But she and her husband were not well off, and the rest of my childhood was one of deprivation, wearing the cast-offs of older cousins, attending a local High School, with no foreign holidays or riding, and the doors of the county houses, where I had been received with my parents on equal terms, suddenly and finally closed.

At Ruskin I was happy again at last, more so indeed than ever before. I was sure that I was going to do great things, an opinion shared to some extent by the professors. This may have been due to sheer euphoria on my part, at finding myself in congenial surroundings, doing what I wanted to do and surpassing, without too much effort, most of the other students.

15

On theirs, perhaps it was wishful thinking, an over-eagerness to find some original talent among the industrious plodders they struggled with every day. Whatever the cause, we were all most woefully wrong. For a year or so after leaving the College I worked away, spoiling one canvas after another, unhappily aware that each was worse than the last, commonplace, derivative, lifeless; and I sold nothing at all. Presently my money was gone and there was no help for it but to look for a job; and I, who was to have been another Manet or Sisley, landed up in the Lord Chesterfield Comprehensive School.

It seemed a great piece of luck at the time, because everywhere else I had tried, starting high and working gradually down, had been barred to me for lack of teaching experience. Art schools, polytechnics, evening classes, all had refused me and I was on the brink of despair. At the Lord Chesterfield, however, no one asked what I had done before or even precisely what my qualifications were. The questions put to me chiefly related to my stamina, moral and physical, as if I were seeking to join a mountaineering or polar expedition. My answers proving satisfactory, I was appointed, and then, of course, I soon found out the reason for this approach.

How strange it is to reflect that, without my providential win, I should have spent the rest of my working life in that hellhole, or in others like it! For thirty years and more, morning and evening in term-time, I should have queued in all weathers for a bus or squeezed with countless others into a Tube, lunched in a sordid canteen or snackbar, passed my days in a hot, smelly, noisy classroom, achieving little or nothing, with little or nothing to look forward to or back on. Mysterious indeed are the workings of fate: there I suddenly was, rich by any standard, my sufferings at an end and myself without a care for the future.

I found my charming flat in this exclusive neighbourhood: I made new friends and took up again with some of my childhood ones: I kept a horse at livery and rode in the Park. I lived in the manner already described. My rooms were always full of flowers. It was comical how some of my previous habits died hard. In the early days I would still mechanically steam an unused stamp off an envelope or wring the last half-inch of toothpaste from its tube; but, as time went by, I gradually settled to the new way of life as if I had never known a different one.

And now this stranger from the flat next door had to come bursting in and, with just a very few words, fill my mind with all sorts of anxious foreboding and dark imagination. For a while longer I sat there fretting and then decided to calm my spirits, if possible, by taking a turn in the Park. All desire for supper had gone, and in any case the Schnitzel was burnt to a cinder.

•

I walked to the Round Pond and paused awhile to watch the boys sailing their model boats and the dogs of every size and breed splashing in and out of the water. Then I wandered over the grass, under the tall trees, along by the borders with the carefully tended shrubs and, at this time of year, a fiery burst of roses. As a rule I would spend a long time at them, drinking their beauty in, comforted to find something in London still properly seen to; but now, deep in my thoughts, I paid little attention to what went on around me. An American dowager asked for the way to Peter Pan and I walked dreamily past her as if she had not spoken, only becoming aware of her question when I was too far off to reply.

Gradually, however, with the exercise and the gentle warmth of the air, the disagreeable effect of Cruise's words began to wear off. It was foolish to have taken them seriously. If my fellow tenants were suspicious of me, they were mistaken and time would prove them so. The ups and downs of my life had made me unsure of myself, and I was much too easily upset. And much too irresolute, as well, I should try to be firmer.

Had I been properly firm with that intruder, this unpleasant-ness would not have occurred. And yet, what more could I do than refuse him a drink, say I was busy and ask him to leave? I had behaved like a perfect hedgehog, and he simply appeared not to notice.

When I got back to the house again, one of the tenants was coming across the hall. I knew him well by sight, a man of forty or so, distinguished, well turned out and with very good manners. If I met him dressed for the street, he took off his hat at once with a faint smile, hardly more than a crinkling round his eyes; and he would hold the front door open for me, or stand back from the letter-basket if he were the first one there and give up his turn. I guessed he was either Mr James Willoughby, Q.C., or Sir Alfred Markham, although of course I made no attempt to find out which. Only to pass him now and then without exchanging a word was somehow a nice thing to happen.

Now, I could not bring myself to look at him. I dreaded to see in his face a confirmation of what Cruise had told me, an ironic glance or some little air of disapproval. Perhaps one or the other had always been there and I had merely failed to notice it. I hurried past him, keeping my eyes on the ground, and bolted into the lift. As I turned to shut the gates, there he was, with hat politely raised as usual, staring after me; and as the lift went up he slowly put on his hat again and walked away. It was clear that he at any rate was not among those who had confided their doubts of me to Cruise. His bearing was that of a man who for no reason at all has just been cut dead. How very provoking it was, how awkward for me when next we met, and all due to that mischievous fellow next door!

And further, when I got to my flat, there was a note from him, dropped through the letterbox. Evidently, I was not to be left in peace. The writing was bold, predictably bold, and the spelling shaky. Mr Cruise had written: 'It was grand meeting you and making your aquaintance, as I feel sure we have lots in common. But my conscience is at me!! We were getting on so well, and then I had to spoil it all, telling you what the crowd here thought. Beleive me, I would not have done it, only I didn't know you'd be sore. I'm writing this as I have to go out, otherwise would have come round to appologise in person. To our next meeting, so! I look forward to it, and to seeing a lot of you in the future.'

This effusion was signed *Johnny C.* I tore it in small pieces and threw them away. But there was something about the orthography that seemed to ring a bell. *Appologise. Aquaintance. Beleive.* Where had I seen those errors before? No doubt they were common enough among uneducated people, but I had a vague recollection of having at some time come on them in a context that surprised me. Illiteracy was becoming so widespread, however, there was no point in ransacking my memory, and the large bouncy writing at all events was new. No, I had had no previous correspondence with the man, and the important thing was to avoid it and all other contact in the future.

Two

The days slipped quietly past. A fortnight had gone by without my seeing or hearing of Mr Cruise again : as the newspapers would say, he was keeping a low profile. And whatever anyone might have told him about me, he must have read more into it than was intended, if he had not invented the whole affair. The other tenants were as calmly urbane as before when our paths happened to cross, my especial favourite greeting me as if I had never cut him at all. I soon forgot Mr Cruise and the turmoil he had caused in my mind.

Then, one evening, as I stepped out of the lift on our floor my nose was assailed by a pungent smell of curry. That was remarkable in itself, for cooking smells were unknown in the house. I suppose the doors were so solid and fitted so well that nothing of the kind ever came through, any more than noise did. Now the whole landing reeked of hot Madras curry, as if an Indian restaurant had opened there : wafts of it followed me into my flat and hung about in the hall.

I am fond of curry, but this was excessive. Hastily I dragged all the windows down to let out the fumes, but they came pouring in from outer air as well. And with the fumes came noise, strange oriental sounds, the wailing of children and a harsh voice chiding them in an unknown tongue, temple music with drum, flute and gong, and now and again a mighty belch. All proceeded from the flat next door to mine, whose windows also were open, allowing the din to travel freely through the square. People and dogs in the garden below were looking upward, in a startled way, and then at each other.

I shut the windows again and turned on the anti-smell

devices, which were so powerful as to roar like a hurricane and drown all other noise. When the air was clear I switched them off, to find that an urgent knocking on my door had added itself to the medley beyond. There stood Cruise, but a different Cruise from that of our previous encounter. No longer assured and impudent, he seemed to be weighed down by multiple heavy cares and when he spoke, his tone was one of entreaty.

'Ah, you're in, thank God,' he said. 'I wonder, have you such a thing as a shawl for the baby? It's more than I have.'

For all the change in demeanour, he still addressed me as if he were somehow entitled to come looking here for whatever he wanted.

'I have no baby's shawl,' I replied coldly. 'I never had any occasion for one.'

'Something of your own would do,' he pleaded. 'The baby is crying with cold.'

'Cold? In this weather?'

'The family arrived a short while ago from Pakistan. They are not used to our climate.'

I should have politely refused and wished him good evening, but I fell into the old mistake of allowing myself to be drawn. 'What family? Whose? What on earth is going on? Why all the commotion?'

'Miss Butler, you may well ask,' he said, with a catch in his voice. 'But be a Christian now, and give me something for her. Then, as soon as I have them all quietened, I will come back and explain.'

'Oh, very well. Wait there a moment.' For I cannot deny that my curiosity was aroused.

I went into the bedroom and opened the drawer that held my woollies, neatly packed away for the summer. The oldest item among them was an evening wrap in mohair which, faded and torn as it was, I had kept because I liked it. Having shaken out the mothballs, I brought it to Cruise, intending to say that I wanted it back in due course; but, with a muttered 'bless you!' he snatched it from me and rushed away before I could speak.

Gradually the uproar subsided. I opened a window and sat by it, looking down at the square. In the garden, people were lolling in deckchairs or playing with dogs, as if nothing unseemly had happened. For the moment, at any rate, our peace was fully restored.

Evidently, however, Cruise had further duties at home, for it was a couple of hours before he came back. He looked more weary than ever, indeed quite spent, and positively fell into the nearest chair when I told him to sit down. I had decided not to give him a drink, but the state he was in awoke my compassion, and I asked what he would have. He said he would 'try' some whisky, and swallowed the ample tot I had poured him while I was looking round for the soda.

'Oh thank you, thank you,' he said, humbly and gratefully, as I poured out another. Once more I was struck by the complete change of manner. He sat a moment or two while the alcohol percolated, and then went on, 'Poor people, they are asleep in bed now, every one. Mother, father, and all five children.'

'Do you mean to say, they are staying with you?' I cried. In the formal tenant's contract on good stout paper and drawn up by a well-known firm of lawyers, it was carefully laid down who could and who could not be received in the house. I had marvelled somewhat to think that in this day and age there were people still who dared to please themselves in the matter.

'They must,' he replied. 'They have nowhere else to go.'

My amazement was deepening to horror. 'Then they are staying indefinitely? But Mr Cruise, it will not be allowed. Are they friends of yours?'

'I never saw them until today.' He leaned back in his chair, absently holding his empty glass sideways. I replenished it, and he continued: 'Wait till I tell you what happened. You would have done the same in my position.' He had been shopping in Earl's Court and was on the way back when he saw the family seated on the pavement, dishevelled, woebegone, amid a heap of parcels and bundles. The father, who spoke some English, had accosted him with the simple words : Where can we go? It appeared that they had left Pakistan some weeks earlier and had stayed in a hostel while the father looked for accommodation. He had found it, in the house before which they were sitting now, but when he brought them there that afternoon the owner had changed his mind. He denied that any firm agreement had been reached and roughly insisted on a deposit of eight hundred pounds before he gave up the keys. The father was in despair, for his money was nearly gone; indeed, he would not have been able to pay the rent until he found work. They could not return to the hostel, as another family had rushed into their quarters the instant they moved out and the whole place was brimming full. And there they sat, forlorn and friendless in a strange land, with no one to help or advise them.

'Can you think of anything more horrible?' Cruise wanted to know, the tears starting to his eyes.

'It is all most unfortunate, certainly,' I agreed. 'But why should you be involved?'

'Because I happened to come across them,' he said, with gentle reproach. 'Was I to pass by on the other side? We are all involved in each other, from the moment that we are born. And there is no meaning in life, if we are only to think of ourselves.'

There was nothing priggish or complacent in the way he uttered these sentiments. He spoke quietly, in a matter-of-fact tone, as a man defining the code by which he lives. I felt reproved, and I was also deeply touched. There is always something attractive in other-worldliness, no matter how foolish, naive and tiresome it may be. I felt, too, how far short of this I would have fallen, had I been in his shoes.

His glass had slipped to the horizontal position again, and I attended to it.

'But you know,' I said, trying to re-establish myself with

23

a commonsense view, 'these people are not so helpless as you may think. All kinds of bodies are there to assist them. The Community Relations crowd, for example. Is this owner, or landlord, English? He hasn't a hope if he is.'

'Really?' Cruise looked thoughtful for a moment. 'But no, he is not. He is one of their own. That is what hurt them more than anything. I saw him and offered to guarantee the rent, but he would not hear of it. It was eight hundred down, or they didn't come in.'

'But what, then, do you propose to do?'

'I must see about raising the money,' he said. 'I can only manage a hundred myself. But, with the help of God, I will get the rest somehow.'

And here again he spoke with quiet conviction of a man who sees only one possible course ahead. I was overwhelmed by such generosity, ashamed to remember how poor an opinion I had formed of him at our first meeting, how misled I had been by the mere detail of an unfortunate manner.

'And until you do, you will give them shelter? I am afraid there may be trouble.'

'If so, I must meet it. There is no alternative. They won't be so noisy, once they have settled down. It was partly my fault. I put on an Indian record to cheer them up, but they are not Hindus and it only made things worse.' He sighed and rose to his feet. 'Thank you for listening. I must go back. I'll let you know how we get on.'

With that, he left me to my meditations.

*

After that evening, the visitors made little or no noise and hardly manifested themselves at all. Once I stepped from the lift to find a chubby brown toddler standing in Cruise's open doorway and staring at me vacantly with eyes black and shiny as two little olives; but, quick as a flash, a fat dusky arm shot forward, pulled him in with a clicking of bangles and shut the

24

door. Another time I observed the squat figure of the pater-familias, dressed to the nines and carrying a rolled umbrella, gingerly making his way down the fire-escape at the rear of the house. No doubt Cruise had recommended their avoiding the usual means of exit.

Invisible and inaudible as they mostly were, however, their presence was signalled by the haunting fragrance of curry. They must have had it for breakfast, lunch and dinner and kept a vat of it brewing all day long. It was heaviest on our landing, of course, but it spread through the house by the lift, which drew it in every time it halted there and breathed it out wherever it stopped after that. Very soon it had permeated the stairway from top to bottom, and made itself felt the moment anyone came in by the street or garden doors.

For this reason, I was not altogether surprised when my outside bell rang one evening and Mr Brooke, the house agent, asked over the inter-com if he might come up and see me. I pressed the button to release the door-catch and waited in trepidation until he should arrive. Apart from showing prospective tenants round, his function was to deal with anything that went wrong : very little did in this well-built, well-ordered house : if it happened, Bert rang him up and workmen appeared shortly after. From the day he let me the flat to this one, I had never set eyes on him; and I knew that nothing of an ordinary nature would have brought him now.

I remembered him as a small neat little man, softly spoken, deferential, ready with answers; but as I greeted him he showed unmistakable signs of agitation.

'I am sorry indeed to disturb you, Miss Butler,' he began. 'I have been ringing the next-door bell, but could get no reply. Can you spare me a moment or two?'

I told him that I would be glad to do so and took him into the sitting-room. We sat facing each other, he primly holding his hat on his knees and plainly wondering how to begin.

'I hope you are quite comfortable here,' he said then. 'I have not had the pleasure of seeing you since we met last.'

25

Well no, he wouldn't, would he? I thought. The remark was so inane, his mind must be busy elsewhere.

'Very comfortable indeed. I love the place,' I assured him.

Mr Brooke drew a deep breath. 'One or two of the other tenants have asked me about certain matters,' he said. 'They rang me up yesterday. It concerns the flat next door to you. Apparently, there was a good deal of noise one evening. As you know, this is a very quiet house. No one has ever mentioned noise before.'

'It was only once,' I replied. 'I think Mr Cruise was giving a party.'

'A party? Oh, a party.' He moistened his lips and stared glumly at his hat. 'I don't wish to be indiscreet, Miss Butler, but have you any idea when his visitors left?'

'I haven't, no. There was some noise, certainly, and then all was quiet again. I assumed the party was over.' In the moment of uttering this untruth, I had taken on the role of accomplice.

'Because the rumour is, that they never left at all,' Mr Brooke went on lugubriously. 'But if that were the case, no doubt you would be aware of it?'

'I don't concern myself with other people's affairs,' I said, with a nip of frost in my tone. 'Surely, the appropriate person to ask is Mr Cruise himself.'

'Yes, indeed, quite so. But I rang his number several times yesterday, to try and make an appointment, and there was no answer. And I have been ringing his doorbell now. The tenants are anxious for the matter to be cleared up quickly,' Mr Brooke pleaded. 'One of them was in the garden on the night of this party and saw an Indian lady, as he thought, leaning out of Mr Cruise's window. Then Mr Cruise came up behind her and laughingly pulled her away. This tenant—I mention no names—reports that he saw nobody leave. And ever since then, there has been this extraordinary smell of curry.'

'Yes, I have noticed that myself,' I agreed, willing to give him what help I could.

26

'As you know, we have very definite rules on certain matters,' Mr Brooke continued. 'Rules framed for the comfort and wellbeing of all. They are clearly written into each contract. Mr Cruise has not yet signed a contract, but is well aware of our terms. The tenants are entitled to expect that he will conform.'

Everything he said was fair and reasonable and correct, and corresponded to what I really felt myself. Yet there was a cold selfishness in it, seen against the plight of the homeless aliens and Cruise's chivalrous attitude to them, that roused my hostility.

'If I see Mr Cruise, I will tell him of your inquiry,' I promised, with a final air. 'Then I am sure he will get in touch with you. I am afraid I can't do more.'

Mr Brooke gave me a searching glance and slowly got up. 'There is nothing you feel able to add to that?' he asked dismally. 'Just between us? It would go no further.'

'No, nothing. I'm as much in the dark as you are.'

This second outrageous lie brought the interview to an end. Mr Brooke apologised once more for troubling me and took his departure, disconsolate. It crossed my mind that I richly deserved now whatever the tenants had thought of me. I still did not know what else I could have done, nor was I truly repentant.

•

Mr Brooke had chosen an hour when the tenants were likely to have returned from their various occupations, in order no doubt to call personally on those who had been 'asking' about my neighbour and give what reassurance he could. I allowed time for this to be done and for any ripples left in his wake to disappear, and then knocked gently on Cruise's door. It was the first approach I had made to him, and marked a further step in my involvement. The door opened at once, as if he were lying in wait behind it.

27

'Sh! the baby's asleep,' he whispered. A tremendous bank of curry came rolling out from the interior, and such of the apartment as I could see looked like Hampstead Heath after a Bank Holiday. 'Can we go to your place? We can talk better there.

'Blasted fellow, ringing the doorbell like that,' he went on in his normal voice when we were safely inside. 'If he'd woken her up, God knows when we'd have got her off again. She's teething, and very fractious. What did he want?'

His face grew dark as he heard of the tenants' complaints and suspicions, which evidently struck him as most unreasonable.

'It's all very well,' he grumbled, frowning. 'The Singhs don't make any noise or show themselves. As for the curry, that is their staple food. Are they to switch to bacon and beef at the drop of a hat? Why can't these people mind their own business? What harm is anyone doing them?'

Diffidently, I quoted Mr Brooke's remarks on the legal position, but Cruise angrily waved them aside.

'Rules! contracts! But these are only words,' he snapped. 'Agreements are purely a matter of form. I am dealing with reality, and very rough going it is, let me tell you. I'm out and about all day and every day, trying to get the key money together, and I've drawn blank after blank. I don't know what the world is coming to. Cost of living, inflation, any excuse is better than none. One of the lads I asked told me he hardly knew which way to turn himself—and he sitting in a bloody great Mercedes while he said it!'

I suggested that people might in fact have troubles of their own these days, but he would not allow it, at least not to the types he was pursuing. Their idea of a problem was, whether to go round Kenya this summer or hire a yacht in the Mediterranean. He'd like to dump them in a strange land, without a roof over their heads or a penny piece in their pocket. It was enough to make you a Communist . . .

He went on in similar vein, with much fluency, his eyes

sparkling with indignation, until he had talked himself out. I then seized the chance of putting a word in, and again spoke of the organisations that were there to look after immigrants and the advisability of turning to them; but Cruise shook his head.

'I have taken this on and I'll see it through,' he said obstinately. 'And here the Singhs shall stay until I have it done. And if anyone tries to kick up, I'll go to your Race Relations chaps. They sound like a fairminded lot.'

It was impossible not to admire him, but my heart sank at the prospect before us. Had I really escaped from the Lord Chesterfield Comprehensive only to find it, so to speak, reassembling itself round me here? And then all at once the solution flashed across my mind, so easy and obvious, it was incredible that it had taken so long.

'I have it! How stupid I was, not to think of it before!' I exclaimed. And I did feel thoroughly stupid; but perhaps it was not stupidity so much as that I still was not fully used to my wealth or in the habit of spending large sums at a time. 'I will advance you the money. We can fix it all up tomorrow. You can pay me back as and when it is possible.'

Cruise's jaw dropped and he stared at me for a moment or two, as if he doubted his own ears. '*You?*' he cried : then, as I bridled a little, he said hastily, 'No offence, I'm sure. It's only that . . . I never thought . . . I had no idea what your circumstances were . . . I didn't even like to ask for a contribution . . .'

'It's quite all right,' I told him, with a somewhat regal manner. 'I will get you the money tomorrow, as soon as the Bank opens. Then you can square the landlord, and the Singhs can move quietly there before the tenants come home in the evening.'

'And you really mean it?' mumbled Cruise, still looking dazed. 'God, what a load off my mind,' he gasped. 'I'll admit it frankly now, I was wondering what the devil would happen. But are you sure now, that you can spare it?'

'Indeed, yes. I'm only ashamed not to have thought of it sooner.'

'Ah, why should you? It was no concern of yours after all,' he said expansively. 'Do you think I could try a little whisky? I am rather overcome.'

He tried a few little whiskys, heaping praises on my head the while, and then said he must go and break the news to the family. I asked if he would like to come with me to the Bank in the morning, but he was reluctant to do this, saying that Banks always gave him the creeps. It was therefore settled that he would pick the money up from me here at eleven o'clock. As soon as he had paid it over and got the keys, we could plan the rest. He then took himself off in high feather, leaving me in the same at the thought of our impending deliverance. Never had money seemed more beautiful and desirable to me than at that moment.

Punctually on the stroke of eleven, boomed out from the clocktower of St George's near by, came Cruise's knock at my door. Yet another side of his character appeared today. I had seen the unsnubbable gatecrasher, the humanitarian, and the flail of the smug purse-proud bourgeoisie: now, he was all business. He took the money and counted it, flicking the notes over deftly and skilfully like a cashier, and asked if I would like a receipt. I suggested getting one from Mr Singh, the beneficiary, but it appeared that Mr Singh could not write and, in any case, was not the responsible party. I then observed, it might be as well to get an acknowledgement from the land-lord, but Cruise pointed out that the keys themselves would amount to one. Having disposed of this matter, he tucked the money away in a strong leather bag with a lock and set off.

In less than an hour he was back, flourishing the keys in triumph. There was a heavy outside door one, a Yale and a mortice for the flat itself, all tied together and labelled *Mr Khan*. I had supposed that my part in the affair was now at an end, but Cruise explained that one last service would be required. As soon as the family was ready to go, he would ring for a taxi and, when it came, would wait in it below: I was to escort the others down and see that they reached him safely.

I did not care for the proposal at all. 'I'll put them in the lift, if you like,' I demurred. 'Surely, they can do the rest for themselves?'

'I'm afraid not,' said Cruise decidedly. 'Mrs Singh is scared of the lift and doesn't know how to work it. And I must be ready in the taxi below, so that we get away quickly.'

'But what about Mr Singh? Cannot he take charge?'

'Mr Singh is even more scared of lifts, and in fact declines to use them. He will go on ahead by the fire-escape and make his way round to the taxi on foot. It won't take you more than a couple of minutes, Miss Butler, and think how dreadful if a hitch arose after all our planning,' said Cruise, in a wheedling tone.

That, certainly, was to be avoided, and I gave in. Cruise went back to his own quarters, and returned soon after.

'The taxi is on the way,' he chuckled. 'Come and meet the Singhs. They are in the seventh heaven, as I needn't tell you. Such dear lovely people!'

The Singhs were not my idea of dear lovely people, and if they were in the seventh heaven, they gave so sign of it. Mr Singh was an oily furtive little man, who looked away when Cruise introduced him, while Mrs Singh, a head taller than her husband and immensely fat, merely giggled and crooned to the baby on her arm. She wore the dress of her country and he had English clothes, as had the six podgy little brats of various ages who fixed me with an unwinking, faintly hostile, stare. I noticed the children's clothes in particular: of good material and design, they had Marks and Spencer written all over them. No doubt some devoted welfare worker had measured them all at the hostel and hastened to fit them out. Not for the first time, I found myself wondering if Cruise were a bit of a mug.

Around them on the landing was a profusion of parcels, bundles and, piled one on the other, a real tinker's battery of brass kettles and iron cook-pots.

'Has all that to go in the lift?' I murmured to Cruise, appalled. 'How shall we ever find space?'

'Ah, we took it all up without incidents. And what goes up must come down,' was the jaunty reply. 'Now off with you, Mr Singh, and wait at the corner until the others come out.' Mr Singh waddled away, nervously clasping his umbrella, and disappeared through the fire-escape door. 'I'll go too,' Cruise proceeded, opening the gates of the lift, 'the taxi won't be long. Give me five minutes, Miss Butler, and then follow on.'

This instruction was superfluous. When the lift came up again, it took me five minutes and more to load it. Mrs Singh did nothing to help and appeared to have no interest in the operation. I was in a fever, lest someone else would need the lift and we should be discovered. Bitterly I reproached myself for having ever been drawn into this situation. At last we were all packed in, hugger mugger, hardly able to breathe; and I pressed the groundfloor button. The lift began to descend, not in its own smooth dignified fashion but jerkily and with a groaning noise, as if it objected to the liberties we were taking.

With a bump that threw Mrs Singh heavily down on a heap of her possessions, it finally came to a standstill. Now there occurred the very thing I dreaded most. The second-floor light flashed on and wearily the lift commenced to rise. As soon as it reached its destination, I clapped my finger on the ground floor button and kept it there. Through the glass panel I caught a glimpse of Bert's horrified face as we went down, and I resolved to rush out the moment we landed, leaving the family to shift for itself. And I would have done so without compunction; but this time the lift halted at four feet above its normal resting-place and nothing would induce it to move again, nor could I open the doors.

We were trapped. The hitherto impassive Mrs Singh uttered a cry of terror, which set the baby off howling. One after the other, the rest chimed lustily in. I rang the alarm, without any result, and then started wildly pushing all the buttons in turn. The lift jumped at each, like a frightened horse, but otherwise would not stir. Presently, the upper half of Bert appeared, on a level with our feet; he was waving his arms and shouting something I did not catch. After a while he went away, leaving me to an interval of despair until the emergency telephone buzzed and, taking it off, I heard his voice.

'You are overloaded, Miss,' he said, 'and you're stuck. I'll have to get the man.'

A period of nightmare followed. Mrs Singh was wailing now, her voice drowning those of her combined offspring: the air in the cabin grew steadily hotter and the smell of curry, mingled with others, more oppressive. How long we were there, I cannot say, for my watch had stopped. Half an hour, an hour . . . it seemed an eternity.

At last the telephone buzzed again.

'Press the ground floor button, Miss,' Bert commanded, 'and hold your finger on it.'

I did so and nothing happened. I could hear Bert conferring in agitated tones with someone beside him.

'Try the basement button, Miss,' he resumed, 'and don't let go.'

After a while the lift moved slowly and as if reluctantly down to a shadowy realm where I had never set foot before. As the doors were opened, with the shindy behind them bursting through and the cargo aboard available for inspection, Bert gave a whistle. The saturnine individual with a bag of tools who accompanied him looked on unmoved, as if such episodes were all in the morning's work.

'What's all this, then?' Bert demanded. 'The lift takes four persons only, Miss. It's wrote up on the wall.'

'I don't think this woman can read,' I said helplessly, wishing Cruise and his charitable works at the devil.

'Well, I dunno, I dunno. If you'll take your friends up the stairs, Miss, I'll bring this lot up in the lift. But you should of rung for me, and I'd have opened the parcel lift for it. This one is passengers only.'

I should dearly have liked to disclaim all connection with

33

my supposed friends, but I beckoned to Mrs Singh to rise from the mound on which she was seated and follow me. The howls of the children were abating, somewhat, and we trooped upstairs in tolerable order. Outside there was no sign of Cruise or a taxi, but Mr Singh darted up, in a condition bordering on frenzy.

'Yess, please, what is it? Where have you been this much time? Whatt has taken place?' he shrieked. Without waiting for an answer, he turned to his wife and began shrieking at her in his own vernacular; and the two of them went at it, hammer and tongs, both yelling at once and quite oblivious of the children and their own possessions.

Bert meanwhile was carrying the latter out and dumping them on the pavement with an air of restrained but deep disapproval. Just then a taxi came slowly by with its flag up and I thankfully hailed it. Still busy with litigation the couple climbed in, and the children followed, pushing and shoving, while Bert and I, whom they all seemed to regard as coolies, stowed the baggage aboard.

'Where to?' asked the driver sourly, over his shoulder.

Mr Singh gave an address.

As the car began to move, a thought struck me and I rapped urgently on the window. 'But Mr Cruise has the keys!' I shouted.

'Keys? What keys?' Mr Singh shouted back. 'Drive on, man,' he called to the driver with an imperious wave of his little brown paw.

Before I had time to digest this singular speech, Bert was upon me. He was a venerable man of distinguished appearance, and got up in his Sunday clothes might well have passed for a vicar. At the moment he was clad in old-fashioned blue dungarees of the sort that proclaim a menial position and, for that reason, have mainly been discarded. Bert, however, had the natural dignity of those who accept their circumstances, and his respectful demeanour seemed to derive from innate good manners. He had always struck me as a perfect specimen

34

of the valued and privileged old retainer that one meets with nowadays only in books or on the stage, and as exactly right for Norfolk House.

'Oh Miss, I dunno about all this and that's a fact,' he said gloomily. 'I'll have to report it. Every fault of the lift has to be reported and a reason given. And there's rum doings been talked of, Mr Brooke isn't half in a taking. Rules broken and all, tenants at him.'

In my haste to clear myself and my anxiety for Bert's good opinion, I made a bad mistake. 'That was an unfortunate family Mr Cruise has befriended,' I said. 'I rather think his heart must rule his head. But we've seen the last of them now.' The words were no sooner spoken than I remembered how, the evening before, I had denied all knowledge of the Singhs to Mr Brooke; and the thought of that gentleman comparing notes with Bert was disagreeable. To the tangled web of Cruise's affairs, in which I had allowed myself to become involved, was added one of my own gratuitous weaving. 'It was done out of pure kindness,' I hurried on. 'Couldn't you let it go this once?'

Bert shook his silvery head in a despondent manner. 'All very well, Miss, but there's me dooty to the management,' he pointed out, but with some little hesitation of voice, as if his mind were not entirely made up.

'Quite so, I realise that,' I said effusively. 'But only think— if you hadn't come along at that moment, you wouldn't have known about it. We got to the ground safely, but the lift started upwards again. It was after that, that we stuck. How sad if Mr Cruise gets into trouble by sheer mischance!'

Bert looked at me solemnly, his lips pursed up. I had never noticed before how closely his eyes were set together: indeed, I had never really looked at him at all.

'Let's go inside, Miss,' he suggested.

'There's Bodley, the workman, you see,' he began as we stood in the hall. 'We shall be getting a bill for his time, and Mr Brooke will want to know all about it. That's me difficulty.'

35

Now his eyelids fluttered up and down, as if my gaze were too bright and strong to bear. '*Unless,*' he went on, almost in a murmur, 'I was to pay Bodley off, with a little extra for himself, to keep his mouth shut?'

I applauded this idea, and asked how much we should offer Bodley.

'Well now, Miss,' said Bert, with that rapid nervous blinking of the eyes again. 'There's his time and his journey. Came up from Hammersmith, he did. In his own car. But a five-pound note should cover it.'

I am far from being mechanically minded, but I was puzzled as to what Bodley had done to earn five pounds. He had not come near the lift-cage itself where, I imagined, any real work that was necessary would have had to be carried out. It looked as if his 'time' had been spent in merely talking things over, and the solution he found, a simple affair of hit or miss; but I was in no case to argue.

'There you are then,' I said, handing over the money, which Bert tucked away in his dungaree pocket, and taking a step towards the lift.

'Miss!' cried Bert. 'You've forgotten something. Bodley will want a bit for himself. It's the irreggl'arty. Always comes expensive, does irreggl'arty.' In addition to the flustered blinking, his eyes were now turned upwards so that only the whites were showing.

A baby could have seen through that. Another illusion was gone. This perfect specimen of dignified retainer was nothing but a finished old rascal. He intended to share the spoils with Bodley, if not to keep them all. This was a confoundedly expensive morning. I wondered how much, if any, of my outgoings would be recovered from Cruise. It also crossed my mind that no further mention had been made by him of the hundred pounds which he had told me he could spare for the Singhs.

Unfortunately, I had come straight home from the Bank and there was nothing but five-pound notes in my purse.

36

'Well, give me two back out of that, will you?' I said, passing one of them over.

Bert stopped blinking and stowed it away with the first. 'I haven't no change about me, Miss,' he said mournfully. 'And what's a fiver these days? Gone in a flash, like it melted. But that's that now, Miss, and you won't hear no more,' he continued, cheering up. 'I don't want to be hard on anyone. Live and let live, that's my motto. But when there's rum goings-on, why, you feel as how you must sort them out. I reckon it's human nature.'

Having delivered himself of these reflections, he slipped back, as it were, into his other persona and, with a respectful 'Good day, Miss!' returned to his duties: while I went up to my flat, to think about the events of the morning and wait for Cruise to appear.

*

I waited in all afternoon, but he never came. It was Corpus Christi, and at six o'clock I went to Mass at the oratory, having been unable to go in the morning. I was hardly in the church before I caught sight of Cruise himself, kneeling before a statue of the Virgin and apparently in a state of ecstasy. It was yet another of his many sides. Wholly unaware of, or indifferent to, the glances of the people round about, he was holding up his hands as if offering her something and urging her to accept it. His eyes were fixed on her face with a look of utter devotion and humility. A bell sounded, the choir and priest came filing in: moving on his knees right up to the statue, Cruise kissed the hem of its robe, then quietly stood up and took his place in the congregation. All this was done with such simplicity that the annoyance I had felt and the doubts of him I had entertained in the course of the afternoon were momentarily dispelled. It was not an exhibition of piety, such as may all too often be seen in the larger places of Catholic worship, but a welling-up of true fervour: or so, at least, it appeared to me.

37

When Mass was ended, I followed him out, overtaking him as he stopped to buy a bunch of flowers from a barrow. His face lit up, as if I were the person in all the world that he particularly wanted to see.

'What a coincidence!' he said joyously. 'These flowers are for you! Were you at Mass, then? A Catholic too? That's nice. What do you say, we try a drink at the Bunch of Grapes?'

I had expected him to start at once on explanations and apologies, and his failure to do so or to show the least concern or embarrassment revived the sense of my wrongs.

'All right, but what happened to you?' I inquired, with resentment in my voice. 'I had a terrible time of it with those people.'

'Ah now! What happened to *you*? The cab got tired waiting and I had to pay it off and look for another. And it was getting on for the lunch hour and they wouldn't stop for me. And by the time I got one, you were nowhere about. I guessed the Singhs had gone, and went after them with the keys.'

'I told Singh you had the keys, and he didn't even know what I meant.'

This came out very much like an accusation, but Cruise seemed to find it a splendid joke. 'No, he hadn't taken in that part of it,' he said, laughingly. 'Perhaps they don't have keys in Pakistan. And when they got to the house, the landlord was not at home. I found them sitting outside on the pavement among all their gear, just as I saw them first, only a peeler was trying to move them on. And getting nowhere. Very determined people, the Singhs, especially Mrs.'

By now we had got to the Bunch of Grapes and Cruise, having led me to a seat, offered the flowers he had bought with a flourish. They were gaillardias, the cheapest thing on the barrow and of a lurid orange, fatiguing to the eye. 'What'll it be? Pernod? Bacardi? Vodka?' he asked, as one long familiar with my habits. 'Or the three of them mixed?'

'I'll have some amontillado, please,' I replied, ignoring this pleasantry.

38

'Really? Are you sure? It's on me, and the sky's the limit,' he said, with another flourish. 'That was a pretty mess you got me out of. I'll never forget it of you!' But he bustled off to the bar, as if fearing a change of my mind.

I certainly hoped he would not forget my share in the business, at least until the money was all repaid. Something in the easy way he spoke, as if the matter were past and done with, was vaguely disquieting. His noble indignation, the evening before, against those who refused their help had carried me away; but it now occurred to me that perhaps they knew him better than I did. I, in fact, knew nothing, either of his means, his character or his occupation if he had one, as seemed unlikely from his coming and going at every hour of the day.

As if aware of my train of thought, when he returned with our drinks he took another, more serious line.

'I had forgotten today was Corpus Christi,' he told me. 'I went to Mass to give thanks to God and his blessed mother for the relief they brought me, and also to pray for you. It was surely a miracle, when you chipped in like that out of the blue. And you won't suffer by it, God will see to that.'

He said this in the unemotional, matter-of-fact tone that genuine Catholics use when speaking of their faith, and I was reassured. I was even inclined to reproach myself for having doubted again. Where Cruise was concerned, my feelings went like a see-saw, up and down, according as he displayed one aspect of himself after another, without respite. I was growing accustomed to the movement already, yet sooner or later it must surely come to a halt, leaving me either up in the air or flat on the ground.

There was a silence after this, as Cruise was sipping a double whisky. As I finished the amontillado, he offered me more but in the way of a man who hopes for a negative. I had to go, in any case, having an engagement for dinner at the other end of town; and we now took leave of each other, with renewed thanks and praises from Cruise and a reiteration of his belief that God would see me through.

39

Three

Next morning, when I went down for my post, my favourite tenant was there before me; and now, for the first time, to my joy, he said a few words beyond the formal greeting. Beside the basket on the table was a heap of large folders, such as were often pushed through our letterbox, advertising plumbers or discothèques or car-hire services or computer-dating for lonely people, and which all would go straight into a receptacle standing near by for the purpose. These, however, were buff-coloured and embossed with the Borough Arms, and each had a name inscribed in a clerkly hand at the top lefthand corner. My tenant had picked out the one addressed to himself, and was scanning it with a frown which disappeared as he caught sight of me.

'Good morning,' he said, with the usual little smile. 'Our friends are at it again, I see!' And, tossing the folder into the bin, he politely raised his hat and walked away.

The chance was too good to miss. It may have been vulgar, it was contrary to the spirit of Norfolk House, but I retrieved the missive and looked for the name on it. The admired unknown was neither Sir Alfred nor Mr Willoughby but Maurice Pughe, M.P.; and this made him more appealing than ever, as there was a Lady Markham and a Mrs Willoughby, while Mr Pughe, to judge from his correspondence, had no impediment of that sort. Further, although I took little interest in politics, I had occasionally read of him in Parliament, baiting the Left with a quiet sly humour that I approved of, and which seemed to go with his patrician features and amused dark eyes.

Well pleased, I threw the folder back into the bin, observing as I did so that a good few tenants had already done the same with theirs; and then looked through the pile on the table for my personal copy, which I carried off upstairs to study at leisure.

Inside was a letter from the Town Clerk, stating that in accordance with the Assessment of the Population Act, we were called on to furnish complete and accurate answers to a questionnaire enclosed therewith. It was hoped that citizens would cooperate freely in making the Survey a success but, should they fail to do so, they were reminded of penalties laid down under the aforesaid Act. A Teller would call in due course and take up the completed papers. In case of difficulty, we should contact our local Adviser, Miss Bertha Mumford, at the Town Hall.

The questionnaire itself, when I had spread it out, covered the top of my writing table. I scrutinised it with growing bewilderment. There was almost nothing, apparently, that the Government did not wish to know concerning the inhabitants of our land. At the same time, it was impossible to conceive how that knowledge would make them any the wiser, or profit them at all. Have you always lived at your present address? if not, how many times have you moved? and what is the longest period you spent in any one place? State your religion, if any (incl. Scientology, Mormonism, Holy Rollerism etc.). Are you a homosexual (to be answered by those of either sex)? Are you a mother? if so, married or otherwise? are you on the Pill? have you ever had an abortion? if you have had more than one, how many? was(were) the reason(s) for your abortion(s) medical or social? Note: the foregoing 6 questions to be answered by WOMEN ONLY ...

For a moment I was inclined to think it a huge, elaborate hoax; but there were the Borough Arms on the cover, the well-known facsimile of the Town Clerk's signature on the letter and, on the questionnaire itself, the name of the Stationery Office Printer. It was but another sign of the times. Once again the fellows in power were pouring out the money they hadn't got on projects of utter lunacy. And they were nothing but a bunch of shameless Nosey Parkers. I began to fume, like any old Colonel in retirement: I wished I were a householder and could have withheld my rates.

But then I remembered the bin, with this rubbish all stoutly consigned to it, and my good humour came back. By now, most likely, the remainder of the folders would have met a similar fate: Old England was still alive in this one corner at least. And this absurd affair had brought me, even if tenuously, together with Maurice Pughe. How pleasant to hear, were those few brief words he had spoken! *Our friends are at it again* . . . That 'our' had quietly but definitely classed me as one of his own, as an ally, it had taken my views for granted. Perhaps my Bedford Row breeches had done it: I was to ride this morning. And the next time we met perhaps there would be some further advance or development.

Serenely I tore the questionnaire to shreds and threw the pieces away.

*

In the Park that day I rode well, as ever when my mind was at peace. An elderly man on a Palomino touched his bowler as he passed and called out, 'Bravo, m'dear, very nice indeed,' and my cheeks grew warm with pleasure. Afterwards, I went to Knightsbridge to buy a dress, with a handbag and parasol to match, a whole gala outfit, soft, feminine and extravagant. Perhaps the encounter with Maurice Pughe was still working away for I suddenly felt that my wardrobe had not kept pace with my rise in the world and that it was more than time to rectify this.

Shopping is only a chore when you have to look at the prices, or choose with an eye to what you already have. I soon found what I wanted and asked the store to send it; and I was on my way out when a small commotion occurred. A woman of Middle Eastern appearance and smartly dressed had, it seemed, been caught slipping a bottle of scent into her bag and now was *en route* for the manager's office with a detective on either side. She was in tears and volubly protesting that she would pay for it, had meant to pay for it, and that her husband would divorce her if they did not let her go. The detectives were unmoved, having heard it all before, and marched along in silence while the customers looked on, some pitying, others disdainful. A shop assistant remarked to another in a heavy brogue, 'I suppose she'd have to do it, God help her, the creature!' a piece of sentimentality that roused my indignation. The world was growing far too soft, I reflected sternly; the proper place for thieving women was in the stocks.

Now, as often happened in this store, I caught sight of some-one I knew, and, as equally often happened, that I did not want to see. I skipped behind a roll of cloth, but it was too late: she was upon me in a flash, shaking my hand and asking how many years had gone by since we met. Her name was Caroline Bigge and we had been at Norwich High School together. In those days she had been an admiring hanger-on of mine and I had been pleased to accept her in that role: it had seemed a natural and appropriate one, what with my artistic promise and her own apparent lack of any gifts what-soever. But now the case was altered. What my talent had amounted to, has already been described, while she in the past few years had blossomed out as the author of three brilliant novels. I did not begrudge her the success and I greatly enjoyed her work, but this complete reversal of our status made me shy of her as a person.

She, however, was talking away in her old eager deferential manner as if nothing were changed at all.

'How lovely to see you again! and how odd, your coming along like that just when I was thinking about you!' she ex-claimed. 'Did you see that poor woman being carried off? I suddenly thought of school and how you used to pinch sweets from the Supermarket! Do you remember? I never had the nerve, but I ate them fast enough!' And she went into peals of laughter.

'Carol dear, do keep your voice down,' I muttered, looking about me in terror. Reminiscences of that kind were the last things I wished to hear, especially uttered in a crowded place at the top of Caroline's lungs.

'Come now, this isn't the Penny I knew!' she said, at the same pitch and still laughing. 'You were always so wonderfully shameless. That is what I found so terrific. You never made any bones about it. Nothing furtive or sneaky, just a quick glance round, cool as a cucumber, and then—literally, in the bag!'

'It was utterly disgraceful of me,' I mumbled. 'I would rather forget it.'

'Disgraceful, nonsense! Whatever you did seemed right because you did it,' Caroline said, fixing me with the humble ardent gaze I knew so well. 'It's not like you to be stuffy. I shall begin to fear you've got rich! There's nothing like wealth for promoting morality!'

I couldn't help laughing at that. Although I had never seen it in this light before, what she said was perfectly true. My severe notions of right and wrong, of propriety, of punishment for crime, my political opinions that grew steadily more traditional, my views on the modern world, could all be laid at the door of the Football Pools. Those nefarious deeds in the Norwich Supermarket, the radical, even revolutionary, sympathies I had professed at Oxford, were simply due to my own lack of cash. But my present outlook, which went with money, suited me better, as indeed did the money itself.

The important thing at the moment, however, was to get Caroline away to the open air. People had turned their heads towards us, startled by her ringing tone: it was clear that most of them recognised her, had seen photographs of her boyish face with its freckled snubby nose on book jackets and in the papers, for their look of surprise changed to one of interest and admiration. I did not want them hanging on her words while she came out with more disclosures, as might so easily happen. Indeed, she was opening her mouth again for that very purpose, as unaware of the stir she had created as she apparently was of my new position as second fiddle. But her unconsciousness of this soon proved to be more apparent than real, for when, hurriedly, I asked was she free for lunch she replied, 'Yes, but you have it with me.'

I may have looked hurt, for she went on at once: 'If you don't mind, that is. I was given a salmon trout and it's all ready at home. We'll stop on the way and get salad, and then we can settle in comfort for a good long talk. Do you remember old Knickers?' This was a trendy form-mistress of ours, so named because she wore nothing under her skirt. 'She has married a Rural Dean!'

It was shortly after this that I realised the finger of Fate was moving in my affairs, had brought me to the store that day to meet Caroline, induced me to ask her to lunch, and her to ask me, in order that certain predestined matters should be fulfilled. For when, on our way to her flat, we stopped at a greengrocer in the Arabella Road, the man who came forward to serve, oily, plump, effusive, was none other than Mr Singh. I had stayed in the taxi while Carol went for the salad, so that he did not see me; but I had a clear view of him, cracking up his wares, pressing avocados, asparagus, strawberries, on her with the greatest fervour and fluency.

'Amazing people!' I remarked, when she came back with the parcels. 'How they do fall on their feet! That shopman only arrived in England the other day, and you'd think he'd been here all his life.'

'Mr Khan, do you mean? What makes you say that?' asked Caroline, absently, as she looked her purchases over. 'Blast! That fellow should be a conjuror. Look what he gave me, instead of the one I chose!' And she held up an avocado, wrinkled, brown and grievously battered.

'His name is Singh, not Khan, and he is newly imported,' I told her. 'He was stranded and homeless, with a wife and large young family. A man I know took pity on him and helped him to find a flat.'

45

'You must be mistaken,' Caroline said, still frowning over the avocado. 'They do look rather alike, if you are not used to them.'

'I am very well used to them, and I met that one several times,' I persisted. 'I have been as near to him as I am to you.'

Her reply to this all but took my breath away.

'My dear Penny, he's had that shop for years. I often go there,' she said. 'And he doesn't need a flat. He owns the premises and lives above the shop. And his name is Khan. He has a young family, yes, but he was never stranded or homeless. What a rascal!' she murmured, shaking her head at the wizened fruit and putting it down with a sigh. 'Now, tell me your story!'

I hardly knew where to begin. Bit by bit, all the way to her house in Holland Park and while I helped get the luncheon ready, I recounted the whole *Affaire Singh*, from the first ominous reek of curry on the landing to the family's departure under my auspices, only omitting to say where the money had come from. Caroline listened intently, laughing at times, putting a question now and then, with the rapacious gleam in her eye of a novelist collecting material.

'What an extravagant tale!' she chuckled when I had done. 'I fear your Mr Cruise has been taken for a ride. And now tell me all about *him*.' And all was precisely what she wanted to know, his age, more or less, and what he looked like, how he talked and carried himself, the kind of clothes he wore, whether he smoked, on and on she went, shooting inquiries at me like a policeman. I could answer these without difficulty, but when she wanted to hear what sort of man he was, I stuck. His rapid changes of personality made him extraordinarily hard to describe: he slipped away as I tried to pin him down, as a ball of mercury will dart from the fingers.

'But do you like him?' Caroline demanded at one point, with a certain impatience. 'Surely you can tell me that much?'

I could not, having no idea of what was there to be liked or otherwise.

46

'A confused picture,' Caroline said, summing up with a disappointed air. 'I should have to see him myself. Can that be arranged?'

She was so business-like all of a sudden, it was really comical.

'I think it can. He's not the retiring type,' I assured her, and followed up with an account of his initial call on myself, which appeared to delight her.

'And there was no cat at all! There never was any cat!' she cried eagerly, her eyes sparkling. 'Fascinating! I wonder what is behind this.'

'Come to dinner one day soon, and I'll try to get hold of him for you,' I suggested. 'You may be able to fathom him better than I.'

'Angel!'

With this arranged to her satisfaction, her professional instincts quietened down and all through our meal she talked in the old unassuming way. Diffidently, she sought my opinion of everything about us, from the overcooked fish and the tepid wine to the dire pictures that crowded the walls and the grisly *objets d'art* that littered tables, shelves and other surfaces in amazing profusion. The dear thing had no more taste than a chimpanzee and apparently bought whatever happened to catch her eye: bogus icons from Greece, fans and dolls from Spain, a couple of dachshunds in red Murano glass, Victoriana, leather cushions and copper ware from Morocco, abstract painting that hurt you to look at, strings of bells . . .

'It was such fun, doing the place up,' she said happily, when I had commended all this. 'I was never artistic like you, of course, but I do think I've made a home.'

That was her only allusion to my imaginary gifts. She did not inquire into my present doings or speak at all of her own, but chattered blithely about our years at school, recalling all manner of trivial events which I had long since forgotten. At times it was hard to realise that she was a best-selling author on both sides of the Atlantic, and translated into heaven knew how many languages, so little had it affected her and so little did she make that power of hers felt. I caught one more glimpse of her other self only when I was on the point of leaving.

'This business of Khan—what shall I do about Cruise?' I asked her. 'Do you think I ought to tell him? He might be fearfully cut up. No one likes being made a fool of, and he went to such endless trouble. On the other hand, he certainly is entitled to know.'

The novelist's gleam returned to her eye at once, with something almost wolfish about it.

'Say nothing as yet,' she commanded. 'Let me see him first. As we were talking just now, a hypothesis vaguely stirred at the back of my mind, which would cover aspects at present left in the air. One should never pick apples until they are ripe.'

And with this sibylline utterance I had to be content.

*

Cruise answered my knock on his door that evening with the Town Hall questionnaire in his hand and a resentful look on his face.

'I have been trying to get you all day,' he said. 'You never seem to be in. Have you had one of these things?'

'Yes, to be sure, everybody had, but we mostly threw them away,' I replied.

'That's all very well . . . Can we go to your place? I'm not really organised yet.'

From what I could see of the hall, this must have been true. Two coconut-fibre mats, a roll of crimson hessian on the floor, and some travel posters of Ireland tacked to the wall, were as far as the furnishing of it had come. There was also a lingering smell of curry and a plastic bag full of vegetable peels, bequeathed by his redoubtable guests.

Cruise did not even inquire what had brought me, but launched at once into his own complaints. 'This had my name on it,' he said, indignantly waving the questionnaire, 'and I want to know how the devil it got there.'

'They all had our names on them,' I said. 'I daresay the Town Hall took them from the Voters' Register.'

'But I'm not on the Voters' Register, I have only just come,' he cried. 'No officials have any business to know I am here.'

'I can't see that it matters,' I said, surprised at the agitation in his voice. 'Why not just throw it away, as the rest of us did?'

'Of course I'll throw it away, but that's not the point,' he snapped. 'I want to know how those people got my name. Somebody here has informed on me. There must be a spy among us. You can't trust a soul these days, it's shocking.' And he glared at me, as if I too were under suspicion.

'But what of it?' I asked him, completely mystified by now. 'Maybe this Bertha Mumford or some one like her came snooping round and got your name from Bert. It's the kind of thing we have to put up with now. Do you really suppose you can keep your whereabouts dark? The Post Office will know you are here and so, I imagine, will the Income Tax crowd.'

'Income Tax!' echoed Cruise with bitter contempt. 'I never in my life joined that!'

Having disposed of the Revenue in this way, he returned to his original theme and developed it with growing passion. Now, he was being spied on and informed on: next thing, for sure, his correspondence would be steamed open and his apartments bugged. His fury was out of all proportion to what had occurred and his language highly intemperate. 'Informers once were found dead, with a label round their neck to say what they were!' he would bark, plainly wishing the custom to be revived in Norfolk House; or, 'We might as well be in Russia, and have done!' He appeared to be suffering from persecution mania, due perhaps to some unhappy experience in his earlier life, and I made no further attempts to argue.

At last the flow slackened off and he consented to try a drink; and after several experiments in this field he calmed down altogether, like a baby that has sobbed itself out. 'Sorry

49

I blew my top,' he said, 'but I had to get it off my chest. What kept you out all day? I thought you would never come.'

There was a mild reproach in his voice, as if I had no business gadding about when he happened to want me. On hearing that I had run across Caroline Bigge, however, and had spent the afternoon with her, he forgot his grievance and was all animation.

'The novelist?' he cried. 'Do you mean to say you know her?'

'We were at school together. She's coming here next week. Would you like to meet her?'

'I certainly would. I've never met anyone famous!'

And he plied me with questions about her, as she had done about him, but avidly and with an eager hero-worship. It revealed him in yet another, and an endearing, light, this unstinted homage to her merit, free of masculine lordliness or denigration. I told him she was coming to dinner and invited him to coffee and liqueurs with us afterwards. He thanked me effusively over and over and then took his leave, having first torn up the questionnaire and thrown the bits away, his humour fully restored.

*

Seldom does anything turn out as we hope. To begin with, I had taken even more than my usual pains with the dinner for Carol and, though I say it, had fairly surpassed myself. We had asparagus, firm and crisp, not floppy, a sweetbread flan that melted in the mouth, with young peas and carrots from the market, fresh pineapple in Kirsch, a cheese soufflé that rose from the dish like a tower of gold, and a bottle of sparkling white Burgundy. At the back of my mind, I fear, was an unworthy little wish to outdo her, to impress her with my skill in cooking as, too, with my taste in furnishing and decorating, all in such contrast to the frantic mess at Holland Park. The flat had been thoroughly cleaned in her honour, and new

50

flowers put in every room. I soon realised, however, that Carol was wholly indifferent to her present surroundings, or unaware of them, and that she hardly noticed what she ate. Her mind was fixed on the approaching encounter with Cruise and all her conversation tended towards him, continually going back over what I had told her before, raising a point here and there for me to clarify or confirm. She seemed more of a policeman than ever, and it was evident that a theory of some description had taken hold of her mind.

'You did say, didn't you,' she asked, absently chasing a piece of flan round her plate, 'that according to Mr Brooke one of the tenants saw an Indian lady at the window and that Cruise then "laughingly" pulled her away?'

I agreed that such was the case, and asked why she wanted to know; but she merely smiled, like a detective in a film who is saving up his exposé for the end.

'Well, I hope you are not going to turn him inside out when he gets here,' I warned her. 'He's absolutely dying to meet you. And don't forget, he's a deeply wronged man.'

'Or a very weird one,' said Carol, and smiled again.

Cruise had been asked for half-past nine and at a quarter-past ten he had not appeared. Caroline, all impatience, asked me to go and remind him, but I regarded that as beneath us. I said I would make the coffee first, to give him another chance, and was doing so when he knocked at the door. This evening he was dressed in an artist's smock with smears of paint down the front and a flowing cravat, tied under his chin in the style of Montmartre 1890; but he had taken the trouble to shave and he was carrying a bunch of gaillardias.

'I am rather late, am I not?' he began nervously. 'To tell you the truth, I had clean forgotten!'

'Never mind,' I said, putting a hand out for the flowers; but he vaguely shook it and hurried on to the sitting-room without further ado. I followed to make the formal introduction, but he took the matter out of my hands, and was barely through the door when he blurted out, 'My name is Cruise, Johnny to

51

friends. You must be Caroline Bigge. These are for you,' and pushed the gaillardias into her lap.

'Thank you so much, how pretty they are,' she said, examining their vulgar tousled heads with a smile.

Without waiting for me to propose it, Cruise sat down beside her and began to talk, very fast, and as if the two of them were alone in the room. He was tense and ill at ease, pulling at his cravat, writhing in his chair, curling and uncurling his toes in their arty sandals, and this was in strange contrast to the assertiveness of what he said.

'I am sorry to be so late, but I had forgotten your very existence!' he told her. 'That sounds rude, but wait till you hear. I have been working on a picture that just didn't want to come right. It is a still life, lemons, garlic and a bunch of grapes, and the luminous sheen of the garlic, the bloom on the grape, defied me. Both have a kind of radiance which seems to come from within, a glow that has nothing to do with surface colour. But surface colour is all the artist has to work with. It was the devil of a problem. I have been struggling with it, I don't know how long. And all of a sudden this evening it came. Naturally, everything else went out of my head and I slogged away for all I was worth until the result satisfied me. And only then did I remember the appointment here. That is the trouble with art, it demands the whole of one's being, makes one oblivious of anything not itself. A hard mistress! but I could serve no other!'

Having delivered this speech he relaxed, as if it had been an ordeal which now was triumphantly overcome, and leaned back in his chair with a look of much complacency. I was greatly surprised, for he had never mentioned to me that he was a painter, and his confusing of Paul Klee with Paul Henrey when first we met hardly suggested it. I said nothing, however: he was so obviously wrapped up in Carol that my mere presence was intrusion enough.

'Well, here you are now, and the important thing was to get the picture right,' said Carol; but her eyes were dancing and

52

the corners of her mouth went up in a little smile. 'Lemons, garlic, grapes—a wonderful subject.'

'A challenging one, too. But that's what I like. The easy things are not worth doing,' said Cruise, with a lordly wave of his hand. But now the oddest thing happened. He was about to go on when he suddenly checked himself, paused in his stride as it were and said, more lordly than ever, 'But now let us talk about *you*. Penny tells me you write. I'm afraid I don't know your name—should I?'

I was thunderstruck by this *volte face*, but Caroline looked still more amused.

'No indeed,' she assured him benignly. 'I didn't know yours till just now.'

The crack popped out so swiftly, it was clear she kept it for use in a recurring situation. Cruise blinked once or twice and his face darkened; but then he rallied.

'You write novels, I hear,' he said. 'I never read novels.'

'Perhaps you don't read very much of anything,' Carol suggested.

'I read a great deal. I am a voracious reader of books that interest me,' said Cruise, bridling. 'At school the teachers said I should write myself. They predicted a great future for me. But Tolstoy said all that I wanted to say.'

'He rather took the words out of *my* mouth, come to that,' smiled Carol. 'But I soldier gamely on.'

There was a touch of mockery in her voice that seemed to flick Cruise on the raw. A wild, almost insane light came into his eye, and he flushed crimson. To be laughed at, or to suspect that he was, clearly was more than he could abide, and his rage was so disproportionate to the cause as to be laughable in itself. Foreseeing the wreck of my party, however, I had no desire to laugh and hurriedly said I would bring the coffee.

'Not for me, if you please,' said Cruise in a voice that shook. 'I have just recalled a previous engagement!'

'Come now,' I protested, but he interrupted me in a passion.

'My time is of value,' he said, stuttering over the words. 'I

53

came here looking for pleasant company and what do I find? I'll not stay to be sneered at by any old female scribbler! You needn't think I will. And I could write her under the table any day of the week!' With that, he rushed out, banging the doors behind him.

'Well!' I gasped in stupefaction. 'What on earth got into him?'

Carol was laughing quietly and seemed to have enjoyed the contretemps. 'Predictable from start to finish,' she said. 'He had it all planned and rehearsed, from the late entry to the artistic ploy. That smock! But he should have taken more pains. The stuff about garlic and grapes and inner radiance came from a review in one of last Sunday's papers, of an exhibition by some Italian.'

I felt my poor brains beginning to curdle. 'You mean, he isn't a painter? I thought he couldn't be. He's an utter fraud! But what was the point? And why so offensive to you? He knew your name very well. And he was thrilled to bits when I asked him to meet you.'

'Yes: but when he thought again he began to feel inferior,' the oracle disclosed. 'So he dreamed up a Great Work as a counterblast. Also, decided not to know who I was, to reduce me further. And when I teased him, he flew off the handle. Oh, I've met Irishmen before!'

'Is he Irish, then?' I said wonderingly. The possibility had not occurred to me.

'Is he . . . Penny, you are divine. You could make sixty Irishmen out of him.'

'Well, anyhow, that's that. Now you can never test that theory of yours, whatever it was.'

Carol stopped laughing now and grew pensive. 'On the contrary, my theory was right,' she said. 'Let's have the coffee at long last, and then we'll go into it all.'

*

'Khan wasn't the prime mover in the affair at all,' Carol began, in the detective story tradition, when we had settled down to coffee and schnapps. 'Cruise was. And the whole thing was arranged with an eye to its effect on you. The question is, why? Can you think of one?'

'Most certainly not,' I replied. 'And how can you say that? How can you know?'

'I got the idea from the Indian lady at the window,' Carol proceeded, still in the Sherlock Holmes manner. 'Cruise, you remember, "laughingly pulled her away". He would not have done that if he had not known her well. The yarn of his finding them on the pavement was all cock and bull. But why, why go to such lengths, merely to make an impression on you?'

I felt that the dear girl was racing on a deal too fast.

'Is that all? His pulling her away? He might have done it without thinking. It was important for her not to be seen,' I argued. 'And whether Khan had told him the truth or not, Cruise certainly believed him. He was awfully upset about it, went all over the place trying to raise the money.'

'Or so he said,' Carol put in.

'You are a suspicious woman!' I laughed; but I was feeling a little annoyed. 'Well, since you are so clever, go ahead and explain the whole thing.'

'That's just what I can't do. I can't see where you come in. You are the key to the whole business, and there seems no earthly reason why you should be. Evidently Cruise wanted you to think well of him, but that is hardly enough.'

'Carol the whole thing is fantastic. Khan and Cruise in cahoots, myself the key to it—and all simply because you choose to interpret Mrs Kahn's being pulled from the window in a certain way. You would never do for Scotland Yard!'

'Well, I've done what I could. We shall have to leave it,' said Carol, leaning back comfortably as if the matter were closed. 'But it's not a question of *simply because*. I got the idea the first time you told me, and I knew it was right the moment I saw Cruise.'

55

'How?'

'How? I recognised him, that's how,' said Carol, in an off-hand tone. 'A few days before I met you in Knightsbridge I went past the Khans' shop and Cruise was inside, talking to Khan and laughing his head off.'

It is said that a man hit by a bullet feels nothing at first but the sharp knock at the moment of penetration. In like manner, Carol's words went through my ears to my brain without producing any immediate effect. She spoke so casually, and so plainly regarded this as a minor part of the story, that I merely nodded and said, 'Aha.' Then suddenly, as with the wounded, realisation of the case rushed in upon me: the ground seemed to give way, my head spun and I was fit to choke with rage. Cruise's perfidy was too immense, too ramified, for me to grasp at a blow and the feature.of it I singled out was not even the one that appalled me most.

In a strangled voice I cried, 'My eight hundred pounds!'

Carol was reanimated at once, and sat up straight with shining eyes. 'The missing link! I knew there was something,' she exclaimed in triumph. 'It was all an elaborate confidence trick. The man is a bit of an artist, after all. But why did you keep this dark?' she rounded on me. 'It was the most important part of the story.'

'I . . . I didn't like to,' I said lamely. In fact, it had never struck me as relevant. At no time had I entertained any suspicion of Cruise and, throughout, had acted like the perfect mug I had suspected him of being himself.

Carol smiled and became her old fond self again. 'You don't change, do you?' she said, gently stroking my hand. 'You were always the little lady!'

I had never felt less like one in all my days. My thoughts were purely of revenge. They distracted me to the point where I could hardly talk with coherence. Noticing it, Carol said I must be tired and should go to bed. There was a motherly concern in her manner, and also a touch of awe, as if simpletons like me had never crossed her path hitherto. To fill my

56

cup to the brim, she then urged me to take no steps in the matter without consulting her.

'I know what you must think,' I said glumly. 'But you didn't hear Cruise talking, almost with tears in his eyes, and borrowing a shawl for the poor little homeless baby, and carrying on about the heartless bourgeoisie. And giving thanks to the Virgin!' I cried, with a sudden access of fury. Out of shyness with the Protestant Carol I had not spoken of this before, but I now recounted to her the scene at the Oratory. 'The man's a monster!'

'I suppose a criminal can return thanks like anyone else when he pulls something off,' said Carol. 'Criminals are often devout, as most people are who live dangerously. But, excuse me, Penny, it was a shocking amount of money. Are you all right? I've just got some royalties . . .'

'Oh that's the least of my worries, thanks very much all the same. I won't even miss it.'

She was too polite to question me further, but I saw she was puzzled.

'I was wondering why Cruise should have fixed on you,' she said presently. 'He must somehow have known what your circumstances were.'

'He couldn't have done. Nobody does. I came unexpectedly into money, and I never breathed a word to a soul.'

'Mystery on every side,' said Carol. 'Well, to bed with you now and try not to think about it. I'm off.'

I went down with her to the hall and we said goodnight. During my brief absence a note had been pushed under the door of my flat and, taking it up, I recognised the flamboyant hand of Cruise: indeed, he had written with so many flourishes that I could hardly read the text and the signature looked like a whirlpool. He complained of his treatment in my house and demanded a written 'appology', failing which he must regretfully consider our 'aquaintance' at an end.

Four

It was hours before I got to bed that night. I paced up and down like a captive bear, stood with my burning forehead pressed to the window, fell to pacing again, had a drink, fussed with the debris of the party, picked things up and dropped them, hardly conscious of what I was doing or why. Try not to think of it, Carol had said—as if I could help myself! It was not so much the coldblooded fraud or the loss of the money as the ease with which it had all been done. Looking back now that it was over, I saw but too clearly the pointers that should have put me on guard: Cruise's preliminary visit, with no conceivable motive but to size me up: his impudence then, so incompatible with the sensitive compassionate person he later set up to be; and the very idea of his proposing to collect so large a sum and for such a purpose from random acquaintances, who naturally would have declined. Yet I had swallowed the whole fantastic saga, had boggled at nothing, and the humiliation was so intense that it was like a physical pain.

After a while, I began to dream of vengeance again. To pay him out in full, and savagely, seemed the only way to recover my self-respect. The trouble was, there appeared to be nothing that I could do. I could not even sue for the return of the money, there being no proof of his having received it. He must have known when he offered me a receipt that I should be fool enough to refuse. If I went to the police without one, they would only laugh, and in any case I did not relish the prospect of my folly being known to the world. No doubt, Cruise had foreseen that too: he had me nicely sewn up altogether. My

58

thoughts went round and round, churning away and getting nowhere, until at last I went to bed and dozed fitfully on and off until the morning.

As if my unconscious mind had been working on through my sleep, I woke in a different mood. Instead of that wild but indefinite yearning to get even, there was a grim resolve to do it. And this was in every way beneficial, giving me what I had lacked for so long, a real purpose in life. It showed itself in my breakfasting off an egg, as one with work to do, instead of the usual cup of black coffee. A second departure was to leave the house as soon as my cleaner arrived. This woman, Mrs Bird, came to me three times a week and from the moment she opened the door released a flood of talk at me, all to do with her family. She regarded this as her right, like surplus food or cast-off clothing, and up to now I had never denied it to her. Today as she entered, bursting with news of her Syd and her Doris, she found me dressed and ready to go; and she had perforce to content herself with firing some items after me as I made for the lift.

The break with routine had a tonic effect on my spirits and I walked briskly round the square, enjoying the early morning freshness and planning the start of my campaign. Before anything else, I decided, it must be brought home to Cruise that the cat was out of the bag. Even his colossal assurance could hardly withstand the shock of that. He could never divine the coincidences that had given his secret away: it would be inexplicable, almost uncanny, and his guilty mind would be full of terror as he waited to see what would happen next.

The problem was, how to achieve this end in the cruellest manner. I could of course answer his impudent note of the night before with one that would act as a bombshell. He would open it with complacency, the coxcomb, expecting to find his 'appology' and scarcely able to believe his eyes as he read. There was balm in the very idea and I was disposed to carry it out; but then I realised that this would be a declaration of war and that I would have shown my hand. For a fellow of Cruise's agile wits, to know where he stood must be half the battle : whereas if the news were to reach him in some round-about way, his own paranoiac cast of mind would help to unnerve him.

Having reasoned this through, I began to consider methods and presently hit on one that struck me as simple, bold and brilliant. This was to go round to the greengrocer's shop in the Arabella Road and confront Mr Khan. Nothing was to be said, of course. There was no telling how far, if at all, he had involved himself in the swindle. But he had been introduced to me as a newcomer to the country, homeless and in need of succour. He was now to stand before me exposed, the pro-prietor of a flourishing business, well dug in and in need of nothing at all. I fairly smacked my lips at the thought of the rogue's discomfiture and of what he would say to Cruise.

There was no one but Khan in the shop when I got there and I studied him for a while through the window. He was at work on a tray of strawberries, turning them about so that bruises and slug-holes could not be seen. When he had finished this, he stepped back and considered the effect with an artist's pride. Next, he flitted to and fro, changing prices, as if inflation had been steadily creeping up while he saw to the berries. Next, he picked up a melon and shook it beside his ear with a dreamy expression : took a thoughtful bite from a pear, nodded his head in approval, and replaced the fruit, unbitten side to the world; and then, with a brush, he swept up a few tomatoes that were spilled on the floor and broken, and arranged them in a punnet.

Unaware of the enemy at his gate, he carried out these simple tasks, engrossed as a child. You could see that here was a man who loved his calling. There was something so innocent and happy about him, he was so utterly at home with himself, that it seemed inhuman to shatter his peace of mind. Yet it had to be done, if my strategy were to succeed; and I now stepped into the doorway, opening fire without further loss of time.

'Good morning, Mr Khan,' I said. 'Will you please direct me to the nearest police station?'

That was all. According to the plan, the sight of me plus the mention of police should have thrown him into a panic. I had anticipated protestations, excuses, appeals for mercy, even tears, but he merely looked up from his tomatoes and beamed, uncovering a set of large gold teeth that dazzled the eye.

'This fruit shop here,' he smiled, without batting an eyelid. 'No polissman here.'

'I realise that, Mr *Khan*.' The emphasis on his real name was thrown away, for he did not flinch. 'I asked you, where the nearest police station was.'

'This fruit shop, please,' he repeated, amiably. 'Soon will be delicatessen too, for Indian specialitee. But not poliss station, no. That not business for me.'

It could only be that, to him, all Englishwomen looked alike. It seemed absurd, because I am hardly run of the mill. My colouring marks me out, as my hair is a warm blonde but my brows and lashes a deep brown, as if belonging to someone else; and my eyes are prominent and very blue. But unless he were the finest actor on earth, Khan really did not know me. The word 'police', which I had intended as a kind of depth charge, had not rattled him in the slightest. My little ruse had completely misfired.

It was a pity I didn't retire in good order at once, but the role allotted to Khan in my scheme was crucial. I now determined to try the approach direct. Advancing further into the shop, I looked him full in the eye—or rather attempted to do so, for his eyeballs slithered about in his head as if they had come away from their moorings—and began: 'Haven't I had the pleasure of meeting you somewhere before . . .'

Khan rose on the tips of his little pointed shoes and signalled wildly to someone beyond in the street. A bearded young policeman halted in his tracks and stared through the window, first at Khan and then at me, judiciously, sizing things up, before moving with a resolute air towards us.

'Now then, what's going on here?' he asked, frowning. 'Someone annoyed you, sir?' And he looked severely in my direction.

'Yess, please, no, here is lady for poliss,' chirruped Mr Khan, flashing his golden smile again.

'I am surprised at you, Miss, that looks to be an educated young lady,' the policeman said, producing a notebook. 'Now, sir, what's the complaint?'

'I was only inquiring the way to a police station,' I said crossly.

Mr Khan looked as pleased as if I had taken a whole tray of rotten strawberries off his hands.

'Why come in here for that?' demanded the officer of the law acutely. 'Sounds thin to me. Sounds like *harassment*, that does, asking a fruiterer where the police station is. There's too much of this kind of thing. All because he's an overseas gentleman. Why not ask the butcher over the way?' He jerked his thumb towards *Albert Bunce, Victualler*, where a man with carroty hair and a gnarled purple face was sawing away at a side of beef. 'Ah. Not likely! Well, then.'

Mr Khan now gallantly came to the rescue. 'Lady correct, she did ask for station,' he confirmed. 'Then you come by, so I can save her trouble.'

There was a pause while the policeman struggled to adjust his ideas. 'And what did you want the station *for*?' he rapped out then, determined to catch me somewhere.

Having never considered the point, I was completely at a loss. What did people want police stations for? I had not, so far, ever been inside one, and hardly knew what happened there. The policeman's accusing manner deprived me of the power to think, but he was expecting an answer. I should have to say something, however feeble, and I came up with the first unfortunate notion that struck me.

'I found a five pound note in the gutter just now, and wanted to hand it in.'

At this, Mr Khan opened wide his arms and clapped his

little paws together in ecstasy. 'Mine! please, it is mine!' he shrieked. 'I did lose one there on the way back from market, but I could not leave shopp and go looking. This very wonderful thing.' He called out joyously in his own vernacular and Mrs Khan emerged from some lair, carrying the baby, wrapped in my borrowed stole. She too gave no sign of recognition, but her face lit up as her husband chattered on, and she came across to me, smiling and nodding, and gently stroked my arm. The policeman grudgingly unbent, remarking that all was well that ended well, he liked to see things come right and life was full of coincidence.

By the mercy of heaven, I had some fivers about me. There was nothing for it but to hand one over to Mr Khan, who waved it above his oily head in glee before dashing it into the leathern pouch at his waist. And so my masterly tentative ended in utter, inglorious, defeat. Khan had made rings round me, as he probably did round all but a gifted few exactly like him.

I looked for a crumb of comfort in the very way he had brought it off. The business of the fiver had been sprung on him out of the blue and he had reacted with the speed of light: surely, then, to recognise me and decide what to do would also have taken him but a split second? And surely, his shrieks to Mrs Khan had included a warning? Surely she must have known me again, after our long imprisonment in the lift? Might it, after all, not come to Cruise's ears and terrify him? But I did not really believe this. No human being could have put on a performance like that. He had not known me. He had forgotten me the moment I ceased to figure in his affairs. And I determined to give him a wide berth from this day on. Anything to do with the Khans seemed to involve a parting with five pound notes.

*

I decided to go home on foot, so that Mrs Bird would finish

her work and leave before I got there. Her monologue, at this moment, would be the very last straw. Presently I came to the Borough Town Hall, which reminded me of the questionnaire and its amazing effect on Cruise. He had not been acting then, of that I felt sure. For all his brazen assurance, he went in fear of some kind, unfounded perhaps but real to him. What could be more to the purpose than to play on this fear, keep it alive, to the detriment, even the crack-up, of his morale? That would be true psychological warfare. It was my second brilliant idea that morning and one, this time, that could hardly fail. My good humour restored, I went inside the building to recon-noitre.

I had been in a few such places before, and as I remembered them they always had a solitary man, often one-armed or wooden-legged and with campaign ribbons on his tunic, at the door, who directed people to the various offices without delay. Now all such quaint survivals had apparently been abolished. Two young men, with hair about their shoulders, who were lounging against the wall, could tell me nothing. It was not their job to do so, they said: inquiries were handled by the Information Centre. This was a spacious room, containing half a dozen clerks, each with a desk and telephone, and a long table down the middle on which were spread an assortment of leaflets and brochures. There was also a heap of plastic bags, for issue free of charge to householders whenever, as usual, the dustmen were on strike. At this particular hour a trolley was going from desk to desk, depositing a beaker of greyish liquid and a couple of doughnuts on each. No one contemplating this peaceful scene would have imagined that the Borough was thousands and thousands of pounds in the red.

I went to the desk at the end of the row and inquired for Miss Bertha Mumford, who figured in the questionnaire as the 'contact' for those in trouble. The clerk had taken a huge bite of bun and his cheek was swollen as if by a boil; his only reply was a muffled 'Fearch me!' from which I deduced that Miss Mumford was not his pigeon. The next beside him was a girl who said, without looking up, that I had better consult the third, a Negro. He too lacked information and on my showing signs of annoyance growled like an angry dog. At the fourth and fifth, I drew blanks again. Each of them must have had his own little field of inquiry, taking no interest whatever in what lay beyond it.

With five of them eliminated, it had to be the sixth or nothing. He was wholly taken up with the scum on his coffee, which he was trying to remove with a pencil, and ignored me altogether until this was done to his satisfaction. He then dipped a doughnut in the beaker, took a bite with obvious relish and said that Miss Mumford was not available.

'She's locked herself in,' he revealed, munching. 'They're all after her, poor thing.'

'A friend of mine wants help with his questionnaire.'

'Better come round himself, then, hadn't he? But she won't see him,' he said, immersing the doughnut again. 'Blow me down!' he cried in exasperation as he drew it out with a trail of scum adhering, 'what's got into the coffee today? Worse than a duck-pond.'

'It says, to contact her in case of difficulty.'

'Ah, that's what it *says*. Only, they never knew there'd be such a mob,' he said vaguely, intent on his own concerns. 'Turning nasty and all. Threats. I suppose you wouldn't have such a thing as a spoon about you?'

'Of course I haven't. And I want to speak to someone in authority, please,' I said, in my grimmest classroom manner.

'You might have had,' said the clerk, aggrieved. 'Some do. It's nothing unreasonable.'

The wretch was so impervious, he might almost have been in Cruise's pay. It really looked as if my second plan would founder like the first. 'Did you, or did you not, hear me say I wished to speak to someone in authority?' I rapped out.

'Nature of business?'

'To lodge a complaint.'

65

'Complaint! There's nothing but, these days,' he cried, flaring up. 'About me, I daresay. This is my coffee break. If I worked anywhere decent, instead of this rotten old Town Hall, I wouldn't be here. I should be in a canteen. One can't have even a cup of coffee in peace.'

As he delivered this speech, his voice grew louder and louder until by the end it was a roar, shattering the repose of his colleagues. There was an angry hum of support for him and censure for me. Badgering people at coffee time! talking of complaint! who did I think I was? Gratified by their loyalty, the spokesman for Miss Mumford mounted a further attack. 'Said she had come on behalf of a friend, a likely story!' He reckoned I was one of these snoopers, sent by a Tory paper to stir up trouble, like that fellow the other day, with his *Rest Cure at the Borough Town Hall*. They'd be reading all about it again, how nothing was done here except waste the public money.

The affront to which he referred must have been fresh in their minds and rankling still, for now they all jumped to their feet and started to clamour in earnest. There were cries of Snoopers out! and, No fascists here! The Negro called for a strike and appointed himself the Committee. The girl remembered seeing me on television, at a rally of the National Front.

I began to think I had wandered into a madhouse. Then, with the tumult at the height of its fury, a middle-aged man walked in with an inquiring look on his face. He appeared to be in a position of seniority, for the clerks turned on him as one with a shower of recriminations and protests, abusing me and invoking their union; and he drank it all in, frowning at me the while just as the policeman had done.

'And are you a reporter?' he asked, when he got a chance to speak. 'We don't like reporters here.' My explanation did not mollify him at all. 'You must have done something to provoke this disturbance,' he remarked severely. 'And you had no valid reason for coming. Why should you ask to see Miss Mumford on behalf of somebody else? Where do you live?

66

Norfolk House!' He echoed the words with a snarl. 'I might have known it. I am not in the least surprised. There's nothing but trouble from Norfolk House. No civic cooperation. Irresponsible criticism. It was a letter to *The Times* from Norfolk House that brought the garbage disposal unit out again. I consider that you owe my staff an apology.'

And so this tentative too had come to naught. The vision of Miss Mumford tapping at Cruise's door and driving him to frenzy had been a chimera. I went my homeward way, musing on the snags and hitches and complications that arose to confront me, whatever I undertook. It was all extremely frustrating. I had been taught as a child that revenge was wicked, sinful, unchristian; but no one had ever warned me that it was so difficult.

*

On opening the door of my flat, I heard the familiar drone of Mrs Bird's voice. There was something macabre about it, as if, unable to stem the flow of words on my departure, she had been holding forth to space ever since. But then there came a pause, such as she would make off and on to allow for appropriate comment, and a few muttered words from a man. Whoever he was, the pair of them were in the kitchen; and, assuming that she had nobbled Bert or some defenceless window-cleaner, I thankfully went into the sitting-room to lie doggo until he had gone.

There were various telephone messages, in Mrs Bird's ungainly writing. Miss 'Big' had rung up to know how I was. More clothes that I had bought and that had needed altering now were ready. My hairdresser had had a cancellation and could take me this afternoon at three. It was strange to think that up to last night I had been all plans for improving my appearance and today cared nothing about it. A telegram from Aunt Rosemary, the one who had brought me up, said she was coming to London on business and might she stay; and this too, which would have pleased me very much the day before, now left me cold, even annoyed, so little room was there in my head for any ideas but one.

I rang the hairdresser and put him off. I rang up the store and asked them to send the clothes without a fitting. I wired to Aunt Rosemary that she was welcome. While this was going on I heard sounds of somebody leaving the flat, and presently Mrs Bird came in with her duster. At the sight of me, she gave a scream, her invariable reaction to surprise, and demanded if I was back, then? I confirmed that such was the case, and apologised for startling her, saying I thought that she had company and didn't like to intrude.

'I hadn't no company,' she said. 'Looking for you, he was. The gentleman from next door.'

Her reply literally made me gasp. For a moment or two I was unable to speak. Then, in a voice that I hardly knew, I asked : 'What did he want?'

'He said to tell you, there was no hard feelings,' reported Mrs Bird with a motherly grin. 'Said there was faults on both sides, but he was a little hasty, like. Ah, and he left a lovely bunch of flowers.'

'If ever he shows his face here again, please say that I won't see him.'

Mrs Bird gave me a knowing wink, as one long versed in these matters. 'My Doris flies off the handle too with her young man,' she said archly. 'Oh and she's a tongue in her head my word a real little fishwife but bless you she don't mean no harm up in the air and then it's done with her pa all over again now my Syd he's like me quiet nothink to say for hisself . . .'

The merciful telephone cut her short.

'Is that woman still there or can we talk freely?' Carol inquired. 'Aha. Listen. I have to go to Paris unexpectedly and I won't be able to see you first. You remember what I said about taking no steps until we had talked it over?'

'Yes.' Mrs Bird was hovering at my elbow, her mouth still

68

open, poised to take up her theme again at the first oppor-
tunity. 'And?'

'It occurred to me, you might have some mad idea of getting
your own back,' Carol said, with her exasperating shrewdness.
'I wouldn't blame you at all, but do put it out of your mind.'

'Why?'

'Ah, so you have. Well to be frank, dear girl, I think Cruise
is rather too many for you.'

If she had planned it, she could have found no better way
of reviving my sense of mortification and strengthening my
resolve.

'That's more than I know.'

'Hang it, Penny. I've been right all along so far.'

But for the presence of Mrs Bird I should have exploded at
that. 'No need to rub it in.'

'You've nothing to be ashamed of. I've got a nasty policeman's mind! Which is no bad thing, when you're dealing with
crooks. Seriously, Pen. You've seen the ingenuity of the fellow
when he goes to work. You saw the rage he flew into merely
because I teased him. What would it be like, if he really
thought himself injured? I tell you, he'd stick at nothing . . .'

Here, I drop my pen for a moment and stare bitterly round
my cell. It is not a bad one, not a dungeon : it is airy and not
ill furnished, in accordance with the enlightened mood of
today; but nevertheless it is a cell. I resume.

'He would never say to himself, "after all I asked for it"
and call it quits. He would never even connect it with what he
had done. He would see it as an unrelated, unprovoked, un-
called-for act of aggression and he would never rest until you
had suffered for it.'

'Such eloquence!' I said lightly. For all I knew, Carol might
be giving me sound advice yet again. It made not the least
impression on me.

'At any rate, please do nothing until my return. I hope to
be not very long. My young brother has got into a scrape over
there. I'll ring up as soon as I'm back.'

69

So she was off to Paris, was she, to turn her young brother inside out and collect some more material. I determined to have plenty of it waiting for her when she telephoned again. She was not going to manage my life for me or have everything her own way. She might be a brilliant novelist, but I was nobody's fool and I intended to show her as much.

'Yes if you took a hatchet to Syd he wouldn't hardly murmur,' Mrs Bird broke out as I put the receiver down.

'Will you get the spare room ready, Mrs Bird?' It was against all tradition, interrupting like this, and she gave me a look of wounded surprise. 'My aunt, Mrs Bakewell, is coming to stay.' And off I walked, without further ado, to start making a midday meal. The kitchen stank of cigarette smoke and there was a saucerful of butts on the table. Mrs Bird had evidently held Cruise captive for some little while, suggesting that he was neither as ruthless nor as formidable as Carol had supposed. There was also a bunch of withered gaillardias, and these I placed in the garbage bin.

Five

The morning's post brought a letter from Norwich. Aunt Rosemary was coming in a week's time. She had telegraphed ahead in case I was full up or away. She said nothing about her business in London except that it was *rather thrilling*; but my aunt could be thrilled by all manner of things, from a new receipt for gooseberry jam to an afternoon in a punt on the river Yare. There was a page or so of how *much* she looked forward to her stay and how *delightful* to be visiting Town in the *season* again. She always wrote exactly as she talked, so that her letters seemed to bring the good soul to you in person : the capitals and underlinings served, like the mark in a musical score, to indicate the familiar crescendo of her voice as her enthusiasms bubbled over.

'Dear creature!' I murmured, putting it back in the envelope. Intent on what I was reading, I had not observed the approach of Maurice Pughe. He was going through the letter-basket and, as I spoke, looked round with his attractive smile.

'Well, someone appears to have got a pleasant letter,' he remarked. 'There are nothing but bills and catalogues for me.'

I was on my way to a ride again : it *must* have been those breeches. My heart beat faster. 'At least there are no questionnaires today,' I said, trying to adopt his easy tone but failing through a sudden lack of breath.

'True. That is something,' he agreed. 'I wonder what all that rubbish has cost the country. A question should really be asked by one of us in the House.'

At these words, my whole being was invaded by bliss. That casual reference to the House seemed like a formal introduction. I am Maurice Pughe, M.P., whose name you will know, it seemed to say: I have the right to ask such questions myself!

'Why don't you do it?' I blurted out, before I could stop myself.

It was against all the rules of our establishment, and the moment after I was seized with panic at my own effrontery; but he merely looked amused.

'Perhaps I shall,' he said; and then, to my rapture, unbelievably, added the following: 'Have a good ride. I wish I could join you.'

All the way to the stables I felt as if I were treading on air, and all the while I cantered up and down the Row I was going over this conversation again, squeezing the last little drop of significance from every word, my mind a tumult of vague but delightful imaginings. *I wish I could join you*, he had said. But was he sincere? My heart said, yes. My reason confirmed it. A Conservative Member of Parliament, and with such a commanding aquiline nose, would hardly say a thing that he did not mean. He wished he could ride with me in the Park. One of these days, perhaps, he would do so. He would admire my seat, my hands, my style, ask if I hunted or jumped at shows. Moving on, I saw the pair of us lunching alone together on the terrace at Westminster. And after that, who could say? Our brief exchanges just now marked an enormous step forward in our acquaintance, previously limited to a word here and a word there as we passed. The future seemed to be smiling.

*

I will now say something about Aunt Rosemary and the complications that I feared would arise from her visit. We had kept in touch through the years and I always spent Christmas with her family; but she knew nothing of my present circumstances, nor that I had left my job. At the time of my windfall I wrote her, that I could now repay, as far as money went, her kindness to me as a child and asking for permission to do so. The reply was typical of her. The most incurious of women, she asked no questions as to why or how, but merely congratulated me with loving warmth on the fact itself : said that whatever she had done was in the first place for her *Brother's* sake and then, when she came to know me, for *my own*; and that she would not *hear* of taking anything for it! There had been *little enough* to give me in those days, but now her children were grown and doing well, and she and her husband were *better off* than at any time in their lives.

So that was that. I went to Norwich for Christmas as usual, and again she made no attempt to discover what exactly had happened or how my finances stood. Nor did I volunteer any information, except that I had plenty of room at my new address and hoped to see her there. But even she could hardly fail to wonder when she arrived and saw the elegance of my abode; and I shrank from telling her the truth. Aunt Rosemary was a simple Godfearing woman of the old school and the crazy plebian world of today, where you became rich overnight through—in my case—sheer guesswork, must be quite beyond her ken. The vulgarity of it would distress her, whose frugal ways were due as much to a fastidious mind as to poverty; and she would feel anxious on my account, uncomfortable on her own.

Such at any rate was my belief, based on childhood memories. Children rarely notice much in older people but what directly concerns themselves, and I had never thought about what she was like apart from her family cares and duties. In fact I had no real knowledge of her at all, as I was very soon to find out; but for the present I was sure that my limited, partial, inaccurate view was the right one and laid my plans accordingly.

I decided to leave the flat every morning and go 'to work', so that at least she would suppose I was earning a salary. It would have the extra advantage of giving me time to myself, in which to pursue my campaign against Cruise. What the business was that brought her to London, how long it would take, there was of course no knowing; but I was fairly certain, given her amiable habits, that there would be no awkward questions about my employment and that I could carry the deception off for as long as need be.

To be honest, I was none too happy at the thought of deceiving her, for she was the most trusting soul alive. The yarns that my cousins and I used to pitch, the fibs we told to cover up our misdeeds, all were swallowed with an innocence that finally shamed us into speaking the truth. She seemed not to know what falsehood was, let alone suspect anyone of it. But I assured myself that it was all for her good and her own peace of mind and that, in any case, she would never find out; and having thus soothed my conscience I went to work like a delinquent husband, laying in mountains of chocolate, a sweet tooth being her one excess, and planning all kinds of treats for the evening hours.

*

On the day that my aunt was due, the post brought me an invitation to cocktails from the publishing firm of Dodgewell & Brace, in honour of a Miss Juliet Butler. I knew nobody of that name, but I was on their mailing list for catalogues and thought that our both being 'Butler' had led to some confusion. With the second post, however, to my surprise came a collection of poems by this Juliet Butler, entitled *A Summer's Day* and sent at the author's request, with a note informing me that publication would be on such and such a date and that no review should appear until then.

I began reading them as I waited for Aunt Rosemary to arrive. They were in sonnet form, addressed to 'M. O'S', the outpourings of a girl in love that fairly sizzled with passion. The author was evidently young, extremely so, but there was nothing contemporary in her feeling or style: ardent as her emotions were, the expression of them was chaste, devoid of

74

sexual candour, and the images she used were those of a by-gone day. There were flowers, moonlit gardens, bird-song at dawn, deep shadowy woods, enchanted meadows and, as it were, a hungry but invisible tiger prowling about through them all. The last one, *Death of Love*, concluded as follows:

> Now, sudden as a falling star, 'tis dead,
>> The raging fire we knew could never die,
> The holy flame by God's own power fed,
>> Blown out by nothing fiercer than a sigh.
>
> Oh, never say that this our love was vain
> Though all we keep are ashes, torment, pain!

All sorts of mad unwanted things arrived through the post these days, just as hoped-for letters were often delayed or lost; but I really could not think why these effusions were sent to me, nor what their author could have in mind. I was about to ring the publishers when there came Aunt Rosemary's ring at the bell below and then Aunt Rosemary herself, buxom, homely, a little hot from the journey, longing for a cup of tea, but pleased to be here and delighted with everything she saw.

She had brought presents for me, a bottle of her cowslip wine, a box of her cherry tartlets, that were a grand summer treat of my childhood, and a dozen newlaid eggs, fat and pinkish brown. To get these, she would have taken the bus to Dancers End, twelve miles from Norwich, and then walked over the fields to Rosebank Farm; for nothing was too much trouble for her, and she swore by the Rosebank eggs. She admired my flat and everything in it, especially the pictures by Dufy, Klee and Bigelow, which she thought were painted by me. She appeared, in fact, to be entirely herself, the simple unassuming auntly self which was all I had ever known.

When I came into the sitting-room with the tea, however, I found her deep in the poems of Juliet Butler. That was the last thing I should have expected, for at home she almost never

75

opened a book of any description. Amused, I put the tray down quietly and watched her as she read. Her broad kindly face had a spot of colour in either cheek, making it younger, and the little smile on her lips had something rueful in it, and something else that was not far off complacency, as if she mourned over what the poems were saying, yet recognised and approved it too.

Presently she looked up and saw me there; and then her dreamy expression turned to one in which guilt and triumph were curiously mingled. And in that moment it flashed across my mind that her second name was Juliet, and that she had once been a Butler, and that the business which brought her to London was 'rather thrilling'. I realised that it was she, and none other, who had written all those impassioned verses; and I could only goggle at her, open-mouthed, bereft of speech.

'So you've rumbled me, have you?' she asked, with a little touch of bravado. 'Well, what do you think of your Aunt Rosemary now?'

Then, blushing like a girl, she told me the story of the poems. They were not the late flowers of a talent long suppressed or overlaid by the cares and duties of family life, but were composed when she was nineteen. A captain in the Guards had spent his leave in the neighbourhood before a posting overseas. She met him at a tennis tournament and fell in love at first sight. When he partnered her in the mixed doubles, such was the tumult of her mind that she missed ball after ball and they were eliminated at once. Gallantly blaming himself, Captain O'Sullivan took her punting on the Yare to console her for the defeat and she grew more enamoured of him than ever. She thought her love was returned, as he invited her daily for riding, boating, dancing and walks in the moonlight, told her she was the sweetest girl in the world and asked how she would like to live in Ireland. His leave being up, he sailed away with many a tender promise and assurance; and nothing was heard from him again. Cut to the heart, she tried to ease herself by 'putting my thoughts on paper', and when the poems were

76

written she hid them in a little bureau and presently forgot all about them.

'Three years later I met your uncle Percy,' she said, with a little sigh. 'Then, of course, I put Michael O'Sullivan out of my mind altogether.'

The little bureau accompanied her to Percy's house but, for reasons of space, was consigned to an attic. There it remained for twenty-seven years until, 'in one of my fits of tidiness', she turned the attic out, went through all the trunks and boxes and chests accumulated there and came on the manuscript, the paper yellow, the ink faded, but the words bringing the whole forgotten buried affair back to her memory. As she read them, Michael seemed to stand before her again, just as he was when they said goodbye at the railway station. 'He had a little spot of egg on his tunic, which I took off,' Aunt Rosemary recalled, shaking her head : 'he was always a careless eater.' There was no bitterness in the recollection, really no feeling at all beyond a wistful realisation of that very fact, of how little she felt, of how she had changed, of how she once had felt so much and been able to express it in these words that moved her now. They moved her as the words of a stranger might have done, of themselves, not for any relation to her past; and the thought struck her that, this being so, others might care to read them too. She copied them neatly and sent them to Dodgewell & Brace, who happened to advertise a book of verse in her Sunday paper that week. Mr Brace wrote back 'so *very* kindly' with an offer to publish; terms were agreed, a contract was signed and now, six months later, her *very own* poems were about to appear! She felt as if she were famous already! With that, smiling, she helped herself to toasted muffins and waited for my comments.

My brain was positively reeling. Placid devoted Aunt Rosemary had never showed signs of any life at all apart from her husband and children. She appeared to have no interest in things but as they affected the family. If I were to say, for example, that Venice was fast sinking below the lagoon, she would merely remark that one of my cousins had been there and enjoyed it. Did I allude to anyone in the public eye, she would favour me with Uncle Percy's opinion of him, and leave it at that. For her to blossom out as an author was sensation enough, but as the author of poems described in the blurb as brilliant, of a strange eerie power, stupendous in their vitality, and gut-honest, was beyond conceiving.

'Does Uncle Percy know?' was all I found to say.

'Dear me, I hope not,' responded my aunt, coating her muffin with raspberry jam. 'I am afraid the poems would not be *at all* to his taste. And he much dislikes me doing things off my own bat. It seems to frighten him.'

It was the first detached remark about him that I ever heard from her lips. I laughed, thinking of my mouse of an uncle with his lowly position in the world and his lordly airs at home, his 'I think you had better leave this to me, my dear' and 'I fancy I am the best judge of that.' To hear of any woman's achievement was enough to set him a-quiver with consternation and he would tear a female author to shreds as if he himself were Shakespeare and Milton rolled into one. To find his dove-like spouse in that role might carry him off altogether.

'But can you really keep it dark?' I proceeded. 'What if the book is a huge success? Your photograph will be everywhere.'

'My picture in the papers!' Aunt Rosemary cried, aghast at the very idea. 'I should never *allow* it!'

'Then you must have had correspondence, letters, packets of proofs, addressed to Juliet Butler,' I went on. 'Do you mean to tell me that Uncle Percy noticed nothing?'

'Yes, I do,' she said, in mildly roguish triumph. 'Because I had them sent to me in care of the Bank!'

She was the oddest mixture, this afternoon, of innocence and what can only be called diablerie. That there were depths in her hitherto unsuspected, was clear; but how far those depths might reach, the part they would play in my own affairs, for the present was mercifully hidden.

'So you must be *sure* to keep mum,' she added, 'or I shall be

78

in hot water. Now, my dear, that is enough about me. I want to hear all about you. Have you *quite* got rid of that troublesome cough?'

This trifling ailment for which she had cosseted me in the raw winter days at Christmas had cleared up quickly, before I even left her house. She had asked after it, as after an old friend, in every letter since and she put the question now as if it and her blighted love, her poems, her imminent elevation to author's rank, were matters of equal importance. I hastened to reassure her on the point, and also concerning my underclothes, of which she believed that *modern girls* wore little or none. As soon as her mind was at rest and while she tucked into the muffins and walnut cake, I went on to speak of the plans I had made for her visit. She was happy and excited with them, as a child would have been: our first evening together went off delightfully.

*

From then onwards my life seemed to move with gathering momentum, like a canoe drifting helpless down to the rapids. There were still three days to go before the cocktail party with Dodgewell & Brace. Every morning I went out 'to work' leaving my aunt to her own devices until the late afternoon, and always found her in joyful heart on my return. I had thought she would spend the time, as her habit in London was, looking up her old cronies, buying odds and ends for the house, hearing a concert or two and revelling in the ultimate bliss of the teashop at Fortnums; but she had other ideas. First she went to a sale in Piccadilly and bought a cocktail dress of kingfisher blue. That startled me, who had never seen her in any colour but grey, camel or mud. Next, she wanted the name of a *reliable* hairdresser. She was tired of her *dreary old bun* and centre parting and wished to look more like the Queen Mother. Alphonse of The Arcade fixed it up to such purpose that I hardly knew her again, and now she tore round London in search of a hat. In the evening she asked me to escort her to a controversial Swedish film which, without seeing it, my uncle Percy had denounced as filth and which she followed with close attention.

'Percy makes *too much* of things,' she remarked serenely as we came away. 'Now *I* saw no harm in that whatsoever.'

It was clear that dark new forces were stirring in her soul.

On the day of the party it was agreed that I should go straight on from 'work' and meet her there. The publishers were giving it at the Lombardy Rooms and the reception hall was already seething with guests when I arrived. Apart from a handful of portly men with receding hair and crumpled faces, there appeared to be no one over the age of twenty. A youth in spangled jeans and hornrimmed spectacles came up to me and, in a heavy foreign accent, introduced himself as Mr Brace.

'Ah, Miss Penelope Butler, I am so glad,' he said effusively, glancing at the invitation and crossing a name off in the list he carried. 'Our lioness is not yet here. But all the leading critics have come—' he indicated the portly men, fiercely arguing with each other '—so we ought to get away to a good start. Those there' —now he referred to the milling throng in jeans, ponchos, folksy weaves, the usual assortment of fancy dress '—are all young poets, future poets, would-be poets, come to salute the infant prodigy. Well, Dolly, what is it?'

For a minion had approached and was attempting to catch his eye.

'Miss Juliet Butler phoned, she will be a little late and hopes you don't object if she brings a friend.'

'Of course not, the more the merrier. Vot I vas saying? Ah yes. To have produced already work so mature, so strong, so original! It reminds you of Shelley, of Rimbaud . . . I am simply dying to meet her.'

'Have you not met before?'

'Never. We hev merely corresponded. She is so shy, a nightingale, a Brontë. I wheedled nossing personal from her, except that she was not yet twenty when the poems were written. And you are the only one she asked us to invite. You are her elder sister?'

I did not care for the looks of Mr Brace and rather enjoyed the conversation that followed. 'No. She is my aunt.'

'Your ownt?' cried Mr Brace, aghast. 'How shell it be? Nineteen years old and your ownt?'

'You must have misunderstood her. She wrote the poems at nineteen,' I explained. 'But that was long ago. She must be fifty-fiveish now.'

'Fifty-five! An old woman! But this is terrible! This is appalling!' babbled the publisher. 'We have plugged her as a girl on the threshold of life. Look at that!' He pointed to the flower arrangements of pale pink rosebuds, pale blue Love-in-the-Mist, lilies of the valley and Maiden Hair that stood on every table. 'And we specially asked for the Rake's Progress to be removed from the walls. Here come the photographers!' he wailed, on a keener note of misery yet. 'Vot I shell do?'

'She wouldn't like you to take her picture anyhow,' I told him. 'As you say, she is very shy. Juliet Butler is a nom de plume. She does not wish hers to be known.'

'She has played us a very shebby trick,' snarled Mr Brace, grinding his teeth. 'Hi, Tony, psst!' And he waved excitedly at one of the portly men, who detached himself from the brawling group and lumbered across.

'Miss Singummy here says that Juliet Butler is fifty-five!'

Tony received the news with a complacent grin. 'I said in my review that her idiom was that of a bygone age,' he purred. 'Spotted it at once.'

'You think of nossing but your review!' was the bitter retort. 'What about my advance publicity? Dodgewell & Brace will be ze laughing-stock of London.'

'Nobody reads that bumpf,' the critic assured him. 'I find it all rather sweet. Little old lady. Lavender and lace. Shawls and hearing-aids. Comes on the writings of her ardent youth and lives in them again. Was it like that?' he inquired of me.

'Roughly.'

'Well then! Cool it, Bernie. Play it by ear.' He lumbered back to his colleagues, who broke out in guffaws as he passed the information on.

'Never trust an owthor!' moaned Mr Brace.

He rushed away in search of a drink and, having secured one, started haranguing the critics in a piteous tone that made them laugh all the more. The future poets began to murmur among themselves. I could hardly wait for my ingenuous aunt to appear. At breakfast that morning she had declared that she really must call on Arthur Norris today: she had neglected him shockingly. He was a retired clergyman, a friend of my grandfather, a decrepit old ruin but game and avid for pleasure, who would certainly invite himself to the party if my aunt happened to speak of it. He must be, I thought, the friend that she was bringing with her: at least, I knew of none other. Tottering into the room at her side, or better still wheeled in a chair, he would add a delightful touch to the comedy and fill Mr Brace's cup to the brim.

I pictured the scene as if in fact it were taking place before my eyes. When Dolly flew in to say that Juliet Butler and friend had arrived, I felt as a Master of Revels might, who has devised a piquant charade and is eager to watch its effect on the audience. A hush fell on the crowd and everyone turned expectantly towards the open door, where a resplendent major-domo was waiting to receive and announce the honoured guest. Over the sea of tousled heads I caught a glimpse of my aunt's new hat with its profusion of scarlet leaves and berries. The major-domo bowed and said a few quiet words, probably asking the name of her companion, as yet invisible. Then he straightened up, squared his shoulders and, in a ringing voice which I seem to hear again, now as I write these words, bellowed: 'Ladies and Gentlemen! Miss Juliet BUTLER! Mr John FitzPatrick de Courcy CRUISE!'

And there the reptile was, wreathed in smiles, wholly at ease, bowing to left and right and making acknowledgements with his hands, like an actor taking a curtain call. 'So glad I was able to come!' he kept repeating, as if he were the principal guest and his involuntary host had been on tenterhooks lest he fail to appear. Aunt Rosemary, meanwhile, overshadowed, looked on with bemused infatuation. Presently his eye, trawling the room, collected me and he bounded across with a cry of 'You here as well! That's great,' planting, before I could stop him, a hearty kiss on my cheek.

'I dropped in to see you this afternoon, and there was your lovely aunt,' he confided. 'We hit it off at once. We were chatting away like dear old friends until it was time for the party, and then she insisted that I should bring her.'

'Excuse me, please,' I said, with loathing, and began to walk away. I deserved kicking for having dreamed there could be limits to his effrontery and that henceforth he would avoid me. To leave my aunt in the flat alone with this crocodile lurking next door had been the sheerest insanity on my part. Now he hurried after me and caught hold of my arm. His bewildered air as I shook him off seemed to be perfectly genuine.

'What on earth is the matter?' he asked.

'I wish to speak to my aunt.'

'Ah now, and what is it you wish to say?' he inquired at his most caressing. 'What is it you want to tell her at all, at all?'

He was utterly, psychopathically, shameless, that was the long and the short of it. I decided to take a leaf from his book and, controlling my fury, smiled upon him with all the sweetness at my command.

'Nothing of any importance,' I said in dulcet tones. 'Just to give her a description of you.'

Then, taking a breath and smiling upon him still, I told him in a very few words exactly what he was. No anger, no recrimination or complaint, merely an accurate definition, a summing-up, as it were, of what he boiled down to. Seldom have I enjoyed anything more, and I waited with lively anticipation to see the effect on him.

He did not bluster, nor ask what I meant, nor brazen, nor did he flinch at the realisation that somehow or other he must have been found out. For a second I caught a glimpse of that demon inside, with the frantic infernal hate which Caroline's teasing had sparked off once before, and now the rage, I supposed, of a cornered rat. It was gone so fast that I almost might have imagined it, and then he smiled at me, calm and reassuring as a doctor with an overwrought patient.

'Is that your considered opinion?' he asked softly. 'And are you really going to pass it on? This is hardly the time or the place. Your poor dear auntie, who has come here to be the belle of the ball! Look at her now, happy as Larry.'

It was true that she appeared to be settling in nicely. Her stricken host had pulled himself together and, making the best of a bad job, was plying her with drink and the compliments appropriate to a Dodgewell & Brace 'find', while the critics clustered round and egged him on.

'And then, as I told you, she has taken a fancy to me,' he went on. 'It seems, I remind her of someone she knew long ago. "Tread lightly, for you tread on my dreams," as the poet said. There's no sense at all in destroying a person's illusions. Why, come to that, she thinks you have some fabulous job that takes you out all day and pays you enough to live like the Queen of Sheba. She doesn't—your own aunt doesn't—know that you are a lady of leisure and . . . ample independent means. Ah, but would I ever tell her anything different? Where'd be the spice of life, with no little secrets?'

My assumed affability gave way before this obvious threat.

'Don't try and blackmail me,' I said hotly. 'Tell her whatever you like. It won't be the truth, because you don't know the truth, and if you did you wouldn't speak it.'

'So I'm a blackmailer, too, and a liar, am I, as well as everything else?' he demanded, looking hurt. 'Not very pleasant things to hear. What a difference there can be, in the members of a family! I well remember how you snubbed me then, the first time I ever came to call. And your aunt made me as welcome as my own mother, God rest her, would have done, asked me in, gave me tea and cake and whisky, opened her heart to me, brought me here with her tonight.'

He certainly threw himself into the parts he played, for his voice shook and his eyes grew suddenly moist, as if he were overcome by the recollection.

'My aunt is the best soul alive,' I agreed. 'And even more gullible than myself. I don't know what designs you may have upon her, but if you come round to the flat again while she is there, I shall inform the police.'

'The police! What would a lady like yourself want with police?' he asked in gentle reproof. 'Coming in and out, asking you questions, never believing a word you'd say. But you need have no fear. I'll not come round any more, not ever again. I see that you don't really like me and I'm not the one to push myself in where I'm not wanted.'

With this staggering declaration he made me a low, theatrical bow and returned to Aunt Rosemary's side. She was explaining to the group what a syllabub was and how to make it, but broke off at once as he drew near and left the conversational field to him. I could see that she was, to put it crudely, smitten, conquered, and glorying in her fall. She never looked once in my direction, nor for that matter did anyone else. All eyes were fixed on Cruise, who began telling a story about some friend of his, interrupted by frequent roars of laughter. I watched him gloomily at it awhile and then, still unnoticed and ignored, stole away from the party and into the falling dusk. Only a couple of days were now left of my aunt's visit and I resolved that she should be attended for every waking moment of them.

Six

I kept dinner back for a couple of hours, then ate alone and started preparing for bed. It was long past eleven when my aunt came in, flushed, with sparkling eyes, the flamboyant new hat riding her new coiffure at a rakish angle. It had been a wonderful party once it got going, she told me : why had I run away? And afterwards that *angelic* Cruise had taken her out to a meal. I said she presumably meant, she had taken him. No, he had taken her, or invited her at least, for when the bill was brought he found that he had left his wallet at home. How they had laughed! They had spent a delightful evening together. Cruise was so entertaining and reminded her in so many ways of Michael O'Sullivan that it was almost *uncanny*. The same eyes, the same long curly lashes, the same soft voice, and both descended from the kings of Ireland—now wasn't *that* a coincidence? Her innocent pleasure was such that I could not bear to spoil it and so, like a fool, I said nothing. He must be up to some mischief, or why should he bother with her at all, why make such an effort to win her good graces? Yet I could think of no conceivable way in which she, poor and without influence or connections, might be of use to him.

In the morning I said that our time together being now so short I would take the day off and spend it with her. The real intention behind it, of course, was to keep her away from Cruise. So let her think what she wanted to do, while I ran quickly round to the Food Hall and laid in provisions for dinner. I reckoned she could safely be left alone for half an hour, which was all the time I needed, or so I thought; but I was held up at the Hall by events of a most unpleasant nature, such as no one could have foreseen.

My purchases came to six pounds odd, and I handed the clerk a ten-pound note to cover this. I was a frequent shopper there, known to the staff and always paying cash, so that it was surprising to see her examine it attentively instead of giving me change at once in the normal way. Then she got up, without a word, and hurried off to the manager's office with the money in her hand; and a moment later he appeared in the doorway and beckoned me to come over.

'I am sorry, madam,' he said, shutting the door behind me and speaking in a low embarrassed voice. 'This note is a forgery.'

'Impossible!' I exclaimed; and so it was. All the notes in my possession had been given to me by the Bank the day before.

'I am afraid there is no doubt of it,' he replied. 'Please look carefully at the Queen's head and then at the figure ten. Compare them with those on this other, genuine, note. Do you not see the difference? And now look at the watermarks—' holding his note and mine up to the window '—these somewhat shaky and blurred, the others clear and definite. We have been warned, both by the police and by our Bank, that these counterfeit notes are flooding London just now.'

'But this came from a Bank! I got it yesterday!' I was completely bewildered by now, for I could remember it all distinctly: cashing the cheque as soon as the Bank opened, returning straight home, putting five ten-pound notes in the silver box on my desk where I kept my money, then going out for the day and, this morning, taking one of the notes from the box again in order to do the shopping here. I was so sure of being right that vague suspicions darted across my mind: perhaps the clerk had cunningly swopped my note for another she knew was forged: perhaps the store had been tricked so often that it had evolved this technique for recouping itself; and similar devices, more suited to an Indian bazaar than to Messrs Goodbody of Kensington High Street.

The manager had lost his air of commiseration and was looking at me with a frown. He was one of those little tradesmen, full of anxiety and mistrust, whose deferential veneer cracks at the first strain upon it. My assertion that the note came from a Bank was too much for him altogether, for Banks can never do wrong. It followed that I was not a victim, as he had supposed, but a cheat, possibly one of the forgery gang myself.

'You'll have to take it up with the Bank, then, won't you?' he said in sneering unbelief.

'I certainly will!' and I put out my hand for the note.

'I must retain this,' he said, tightening his hold on it. 'And I will trouble you for your name and address.'

He was insufferable. 'Whatever for? Anyone would think I was a criminal!'

'Those are the instructions,' he replied. 'Unless you comply, I must detain you here and call the police.'

This made me so angry that I was half-inclined to run for it. The clerk had slipped away, back to her duties, and the manager was a wisp of a fellow who could hardly detain a child. As if this thought had struck him too, he touched a bell on his desk, whereupon a burly Commissionaire appeared and stood glowering with his back to the door. There was nothing for it but to yield; but my troubles were not yet over. Fury had churned up my brain to such an extent that I gave my address as Norwich House, a slip that the manager pounced on as if it were the final damning proof in an already formidable case.

'There is no Norwich House in the area,' he barked.

'I meant Norfolk.'

'I daresay! Have you any means of identification?'

All I had were the few letters which I had collected from the basket on the way out. He brooded over them with pursed lips, wondering how they too could be made to bear witness against me, and then reluctantly gave them back.

'They asn't been opened,' the Commissionaire threw in. 'Ow do we know they're ers?'

'Yes! How do we know they are yours?'

88

'Oh, heavens above!'

New as I was to this kind of thing, I felt sure he was exceeding his authority; but my only idea now was to finish with him and be gone. Among the letters was one from Caroline Bigge in Paris, which I handed over and invited him to peruse. 'You will find that it comes from a woman called Carol.' I said wearily. 'And her address is the Hotel Montfort, Neuilly. That's the best I can do.'

It was the worst I could do. The manager read it from beginning to end, with the Commissionaire peering over his shoulder and moving his lips as he followed the text, and then said triumphantly: 'All about her brother and a dope charge. And she winds up, "Heard any more of your confidence man?"'

Even now, Cruise had to rear his ugly head.

'Never mind how she winds up. Is the name and address as I told you? Very well, then. The letter is mine.'

'I don't doubt it,' said the manager nastily, and the Commissionaire rumbled in agreement. 'There, take it. I shall have to put in a full report of the matter. There is more in it than meets the eye. Things go on these days that honest folk would hardly credit. You'll probably hear more of this before you're much older. And I will thank you to keep away from the store.'

As if I would ever set foot in it again!

I have recounted this affair in some detail because, absurd, squalid, wholly incomprehensible, it foreshadowed the even crazier happenings which were soon to overwhelm me. I found myself then as now wrongly accused and condemned and utterly at sea for an explanation. One could not altogether blame this little Jack-in-office: the forged note was a fact, and so was my possession of it. Yet there were the other facts in the case, which have been described. Where could the note have come from, if not from the Bank? It looked like sorcery. All the way home the wildest fancies went round and round in my head, and by the time I got there I felt completely addled and on the point of exhaustion.

*

Bert was leaning against a mountain of bagged and un-collected garbage on the pavement, chatting to the milkman, deploring the times we lived in, just as the manager had done and almost in the same words. 'Things go on that honest people would hardly credit,' I heard him say. From his tone, he evidently thought of himself as one of these. 'Scarpered. Done a bunk. But he was never no class. Bringin in Blacks and all. I seen it right away. Good mornin, miss.'

'Mornin miss. Who's to pay for the milk, then?' demanded the other.

'Dunno, mate. Scuse me, I must shift this lot to the bleedin dump.'

I went on up, considering this little speech. Surely it must be Cruise who had scarpered, leaving a bill unpaid, for no other tenant would think of it. The open door of his flat suggested a confirmation. It seemed too good to be true, but true it was, as I learned from Aunt Rosemary the minute she saw me.

'Johnny came to say goodbye,' she told me. She was looking tired this morning but otherwise was quite herself again, as if the other self that had briefly emerged was, like the cocktail dress, folded up and put away. 'I gave him some coffee, but he couldn't stop long. He was so *sorry* to miss you.'

'He's not really a friend of mine, you know.'

'But he spoke so *nicely* of you, dear!'

I had other matters to think of, however, and I let this pass. There was another shock awaiting me now. The ten-pound notes in the silver box were genuine, crisp and clean and numbered consecutively; but there were five of them. The forged bill, then, had not come from the Bank at all. It had been deliberately placed in the box by an unknown hand. I first thought that it might have been passed off on my aunt and that, knowing I kept money in the box, she had put it there for safe-keeping; but she denied this.

'And I can't help thinking, dear,' she said, 'it is *not* such a very safe place, with all these burglars about. A box on a writing-desk! They would look inside it before anything else.'

'But auntie, I put five notes in, straight from the Bank, and there still are five. And I took one out to go shopping.'

'The cashier must have put an extra one by mistake,' my aunt said placidly. 'We are all human. Poor man, how *frantic* he will be! Do take it back to him quickly.'

'No, he counted them out and asked me to count as well.' I did not speak of the forgery, as that would have worried her for months to come. 'I simply can't understand this.'

'Then it must have been in your bag all the time, and got mixed up with the others,' Aunt Rosemary said, looking wise. 'That's it. You had more money than you imagined. How lovely. I always have less.'

I could have sworn that this was untrue, but I was coming to the point where I really felt sure of nothing. As an explanation, it was anyhow feasible, not utterly mad, and I could think of no other. Trying to put the whole thing from me, I asked my aunt if she had made up her mind where she would like to go. Yes, she wanted to visit Hampton Court, and she felt in her *bones* that the Brown Lady was going to appear on the stairs today; and off we went. The Brown Lady let her down, but she was innocently pleased with all else, the buildings, the maze, the tennis court, her lunch in the open. Michael O'Sullivan, her poems, the party, were never referred to; it was as if they never had been. And I only mention them here because of the part they have played, by bringing her to London at this particular time, in my ruin.

That evening something occurred which I had expected sooner. A telegram came from Uncle Percy, asking her to cut her visit short, in fact, to return at once. He gave no reason, nor was one needed, for we both knew what it was: it irked him that she was enjoying herself on her own, without his connivance and supervision. Hurriedly she put her things together and caught the last train. I went to the station, sad to see her go and thinking hard thoughts of my uncle; but, in this single matter, all had been for the best, as she was spared the knowledge of what was about to befall me, on the very next day.

*

At ten o'clock precisely the outside doorbell rang. The man's voice on the intercom was strangely devoid of qualities, neither pleasant nor disagreeable, warm nor cold, educated nor common, and it gave the owner's name as Bostock. Mr Bostock did not reveal the nature of his business but merely, neither quite asking nor exactly commanding, a wish to see me. I released the catch and he came up, a man of fifty or so, with an appearance to match the voice, grey hair, eyes, skin, moustache and suit. The weather had broken now and he wore a navy blue waterproof; his brilliantly polished black boots were splashed by muddy rain. It somehow did not surprise me when, after apologising with great politeness for the intrusion, he said he was making a few inquiries, as a matter of routine.

'Are you from the police?' I asked, and immediately regretted doing so, as it sounded as if I expected a call from them.

He shot me a keen glance and said that he was, producing a card : Detective Inspector Charles Bostock of the C.I.D., with photograph and number. I asked him in to the sitting-room and gave him a chair. As he sat down, he threw a look round the room which seemed to make a comprehensive note of everything in it. He had come, of course, about the forged banknote, which Goodbody's had handed in together with my name and address. There were a large number of these notes in circulation, he told me, and when people were found with one his duty was to try and establish when, where and how it had come into their possession. His manner was as neutral as the rest of him, neither accusing nor reassuring, but flat, calm and polite; and it did not vary at all as he heard my explanation, improbable as it must have sounded.

'There are two possibilities,' he said. 'We can rule out the Bank. Banks would detect a forgery as soon as anyone tried to pay it in. Either the note was placed in your box in the course of the day before yesterday, or it was in your purse when you went to the Bank and got added to what you withdrew there.'

'It can't have been that,' I said. 'I never go to the Bank until I run out of money. And as a rule I take smaller amounts, in fivers. I only drew the fifty because my aunt was staying here and I wanted to entertain her.'

'Is she here now, may I ask?'

'No, she went home last night.'

'You drew out fifty pounds for a single day's entertainment?'

'No, she was to have stayed longer, but my uncle wired for her to come home.'

'Can you think of any occasion recently, before you went to the Bank, when you might have come by a ten-pound note? Did someone pay off a debt? Or did you cash a dividend at some local place of business? Or had it perhaps lain in your handbag, forgotten, from some much earlier time?'

I shook my head. 'I have no debtors and my dividends are all paid directly into my bank account. And I am constantly emptying out handbags, changing them, to go with my different clothes.'

'Very well, then. Do you know of anyone, apart from your aunt, entering your premises the day before yesterday?'

'No. Yes. That is—only the man from next door.'

'What was the object of his visit here?'

'He just dropped in to see me, but I was out. Apparently he stayed chatting to my aunt for a while, and then she took him on to a party.'

'To a party? She knew him already, of course?'

'Yes. No.'

'She didn't know him already, but took him to a party?'

'Yes.'

'You are sure there was no one else?'

93

'Yes, or my aunt would have told me.'

'Is this gentleman a close friend of yours?'

'No, I hardly know him.'

'What is his occupation?'

'I don't think he has one.'

'Is he in at the present time, do you know?'

'No, apparently he has left the house altogether. He called again yesterday, when I was out, to say goodbye.'

There was still no change in the Inspector's voice or manner, but he now fixed his eyes on my face and steadily kept them there.

'To recapitulate,' he said. 'The only person who was in the flat, apart from your aunt, at the relevant time was the man from next door. That is, I take it, from the flat adjoining? Quite so. You hardly know him, or anything much about him, yet he calls to see you twice on consecutive days. On the second occasion it was for the purpose of saying goodbye. Since then, he has left the house for good.'

I could not imagine where this was leading and stared back at him, puzzled, without a word.

'From what you have told me, this in-and-out neighbour of yours whom you hardly know must have put the note there,' he went on. 'Wasn't that what you intended to convey?'

'Indeed not!' I exclaimed. 'It never occurred to me.'

'But, if your information is correct, it can be no one else.'

'My aunt was with him all the time!'

'How can you be certain of that? You say that she took him on to a party. Could she not have left him alone while she put on her outdoor clothes? Or have gone from the room for some other purpose?'

And then a sudden shattering light broke in on me. I felt weak. Of course Aunt Rosemary had left Cruise while she put on her hat. And before as well, while she went to make him the coffee. He had all the time in the world to prowl about and pry into drawers and boxes, and do any wicked thing that he chose. But why should he, why, why? Had he perhaps not

94

known that the note was forged and was he making a tiny, token restitution for having robbed me? Never. It was a cold-blooded deliberate plant, done for some monstrous inconceivable object of his own.

Feebly, I tried to argue against my own conviction.

'But if it was he, why come back on the following day? Where was the sense in that?'

'Precisely,' said the Inspector, nodding. 'There would seem to be none.' He was looking thoughtfully at my feet. I had the further realisation that he did not accept a word of what I was saying. 'Well, Miss Butler, that is all for the present. I have more inquiries to make in other directions. May I assume that you will be here, should I need to question you further?'

I gave the required assurance and, in a turmoil of mind, hardly knowing where I was, showed him to the door. On the landing he paused and looked at me almost benignly.

'The feet, Miss Butler, the feet,' he said, softly and incomprehensibly. 'The face can be controlled, the eyes look straight into others. But the feet! They always give it away. They won't keep still.'

*

There followed days and nights of torment, such as manifestations by Cruise were apt to leave behind them. I started at every ring of the doorbell, almost dreading to answer. Over and over again I reminded myself that these fears were absurd. I was innocent. The police were clever people who always worked things out in the end. They would patiently track the forgers down, and then go after their accomplices and distributors. And they would inquire into my character and past, and find them blameless. For a while these arguments would comfort me; but then I would recollect what had happened and the crazy explanation of it, the only one I could give. My terror would revive and I would start off on the arguments again, round and round, like a dog chasing his tail.

Nevertheless, time went by and no more was heard. Presently I began to think that the danger must have passed. There was a report in the paper one day, to the effect that these forgeries now were circulating in the south of Spain, brought there by holiday-makers, and this too seemed to draw suspicion away from me. And shortly after that came a postcard from Cruise. It was signed 'Johnny' and gave no address, but the stamp was Spanish and the postmark Torremolinos. He wrote of his pleasure in my 'aquaintance', his regret at having missed me and his hope that I would remember him kindly. He was his impudent irrepressible self, in fact, as if I had never called him those biting names at the party. He also added that he was on vacation and having 'the time of Riley'; and the idea of him living it up in Spain, taken together with the newspaper report, suggested that once investigations really got going down there Nemesis would swiftly overtake him.

That night I slept well and woke refreshed, feeling calm and happy. It was the anniversary of my mother, and I decided to go to a morning Mass. For some reason, as I was dressing, my thoughts turned to Maurice Pughe, whom I had not encountered for some while and in my mental stress had all but forgotten. I suddenly wanted to meet him again, to have a few words that perhaps, as on the day of my ride in the Park, would bring our relations a little further forward. So, wearing my new pretty frock, chosen with him in mind, I sat down to wait for the time that he usually went down for his letters before leaving the house.

Then, all at once, the nightmare started. I had a presentiment of evil when the doorbell rang. I knew, as I went to the intercom, I should hear the voice of Bostock, neutral as ever. He regretted the need to disturb me again. I released the catch and waited, with wildly beating heart, for him to appear. The lift seemed slower than usual in coming, and when it finally stopped on my floor with its little jump and rattle, there issued forth not only the Inspector but a policeman and a police-woman in uniform.

'I am sorry, Miss Butler, but we must have a look round,' the Inspector said, politely. 'We have a warrant, if you wish to see it.'

'Of course not, fire away.'

I was taking heart again, secure in the belief that there was nothing for him to find. Tolerantly amused, I would escort them through the flat, allow them to peer into nooks and crannies, rummage in drawers, pry up carpets if need be or empty out boxes, and tell them I would clear the mess up later. But I never got the chance to do it. What followed now was horrible. Instead of embarking on a methodical all-round search, Bostock consulted his notebook and simply inquired, 'Where is the bathroom, please?' It was clear to me that he was, in the jargon, acting on information received; and, too frightened to speak, I pointed tremulously to the bathroom door.

The Inspector nodded to the policeman, who went inside and shut the door, leaving the other two with me. I felt the colour draining out of my face, and leant against the wall. In a few minutes the man came back with a brown paper parcel, which he handed to his superior.

'In the hot-cupboard, sir, behind the immersion heater.'

I closed my eyes, for the hall and the people in it seemed to be going round in a dizzy whirl.

'You would like to sit down, Miss Butler,' the Inspector said, 'and so should I. Suppose we move to the sitting-room.'

I tottered rather than walked into the room and fell into a chair. Bostock took another and began in a leisurely way to undo the parcel, while the constables, alert, remained standing as if to foil any attempt at escape.

I had no idea in the world as to what the parcel might contain, drugs, bloodstained clothing, a burglar's tools . . . The only sure thing was that it somehow would incriminate me and had been placed there by Cruise. That was why he had come to say goodbye. He had sneaked into the bathroom while Aunt Rosemary, the innocent kindly warm-hearted soul, was making him coffee. And then he had shopped me to the police.

The Inspector was talking again. 'Forged notes,' he was saying, unmoved and unhurried. 'How do you account for this?'

My voice came out in a sort of croak. 'I can't. I never saw that parcel before. I haven't opened that cupboard for months. Not since the winter. Somebody must have put it there.'

'The man from next door?'

Now the Inspector was gazing at my feet. I looked at them too. One ankle was tightly wound round the other, and my toes curled inside my shoes as if there were redhot coals between them. But, in the circumstances, whose would not?

'It must have been. It can't be anyone else.'

'He came in here with a parcel this size while you were out, was received by your aunt and chatted a while, then slipped into the bath room unbeknown to her, concealed it there and left, without her noticing that he no longer had it about him.' All this the Inspector put not as a question but as a summary of my own assertions, and it sounded a right farrago. The policewoman giggled, then hastily covered up with a cough.

'He'd do it all right. He'd find some way. The man is a devil.'

'I understood that you hardly knew him.'

A silence followed. I was finished. The Inspector rose and gave the parcel to the policeman.

'You will have to come to the station, miss,' he said. 'I must caution you, that you need say nothing, but anything you say will be taken down and may be given in evidence.' He might have been talking about the weather. 'Do you wish to contact your solicitor, before we go?'

My solicitor! Dry-as-dust old Sir Hugh, a friend of my father's and a pillar of rectitude! Feebly I shook my head.

'Right, we're off.'

My cup appeared to be brimming over, but there was one last bitter drop in store. As our little party got out of the lift in the hall, Maurice Pughe was rummaging in the letter-basket.

He looked round and, at the sight of me in my charming dress, his eyes crinkled and his dimples came out in the familiar pleasant way. But then he saw my companions, took the position in, and all expression immediately left his face. There was nothing of scorn or disgust or inquiry in it: it simply went blank, as if I were not there, as if he begged to say he could have no part in scenes of this nature. His world and mine were mutually exclusive. He turned away and continued quietly to go through the letters.

We drove to the station in a police car, one of those saloons with a kind of blue bubble on the roof. Now and then pedestrians would crane their necks to try and get a glimpse of me through the windows. At the station I was formally charged with having the notes in my possession, cautioned again and asked if I wanted to make a statement. But I could only have repeated what I had said before, and by now it sounded as incredible and fantastic to me as it would to everyone else.

I spent a horrible night in a cell with two others, a foul-mouthed tart and a drunk. At the magistrate's court in the morning, the police asked for a remand while they pursued their inquiries, and made no objection to bail. But I had to find two sureties beside my own, and I could think of no one but Carol, still in Paris. Aunt Rosemary was out of the question: the whole affair would just about kill her, and in any case she has no money. So here I am in a women's gaol, in the depths of misery and despair, waiting, waiting.

Everyone is kind and polite, which somehow makes it all worse. I have a cell to myself, and they let me buy in one meal from a restaurant every day, with half a bottle of wine. And, as I have said before, I have plenty of leisure which can be occupied more or less as I choose. How I shall fill up the weary hours, now my story is written, I do not know, apart from reading it over and over, searching, as I say, for the least little glimmer of sense in it anywhere.

The Version of
John Cruise

Foreword

I am after leaving the flat next door. The bitches. Bitches, the two of them. Niminy-piminy Butler-bitch. Cackery-Crapoline Bigge-Bitch.

There's no people on the face of the earth like the English. I loathe them. Their voices, cold and crackling like autumn leaves in the wind. The way they look through you, wishing you out of the light. The imaginary peaks they call down to you from. They don't even have to try, it's something built-in, part of their racial inheritance. The women are the worst.

Niminy-Piminy is a lady. She makes you feel like dirt, just being in the one room together. If she didn't know you were there, you'd still be flattened. Cackery-Crapoline isn't a lady. She sneers and needles, like a slut in the kitchen that sniggers behind her hand. I hardly got talking to her before her eyes lit up with nasty amusement—why?

I am an artist too, probably a great one, anyhow better than she. Had I gone in for writing, my name would be a household word by now. I am aware of tremendous powers within me, and always have been. But none of that counts with Cackery-Crap. She values people only for what they do and what they have. She doesn't mind what they are.

I wasn't going to bow the knee because she is famous. My friendship would have been offered on terms of equality. And I did not come with empty hands. I could have given her material for a dozen novels, stuff to put Balzac and Gorki in the shade. The story of my doings in London over the past few months would be a masterpiece on its own.

Well, she had her chance and refused it. It won't come again. For now I am going to write that story myself. Her contempt was the spur I needed, to send me from the solitary heights of imagination to the crowded arena of authorship. My work will combine the power of Dostoyevsky with the humanity of Cervantes. It will rise to the level of Mick O'Brien. And it will wipe the floor for ever with Cackery Bigge.

John FitzPatrick Cruise

＊

12.30 midnight

I drank nearly the full of a bottle since I came in. The bitches drove me to it. It was on the paper the other day, how a man died of drinking a bottle too fast. If I die, it's they'll have done it, whoever finds me take note. These may be my last words on earth. And if I live, I'll be in a shocking state tomorrow. As it is, I'm poorly, getting no good of the booze at all. I don't feel like a man, more like a head of cabbage, except for the roar in my ears.

Jesus, I'm crying like a kid. Would it shame them to see what they've done? More likely to set them laughing, tinkle, tinkle, tinkle, like one of those bloody musical boxes. I must get to my bed if I can walk as far, the way I could start on my book in the morning, after a cure. One more noggin, and that's the finish.

John FitzPatrick de Courcy Cruise

＊

2 a.m.

Mus write this down, most importange. We no what we should be doing, yet do the opposisite. I shouldna open the secon bottle. Knew that, but diddle it did lit did it.

Johny Cruuu

One

I have retained the preface above in its original form, so that my account may be as complete and true to life as possible. As for the circumstances in which it was written, we shall come to these in due course. For the present I will merely say that four whole days elapsed before I could sufficiently collect my powers to begin on the story which is offered below.

Reader, I was a bank clerk. One of a large necessitous family of ancient lineage in the County of Cork, I was driven to earn my bread in this humdrum occupation. Having got my diploma in book-keeping and accountancy, I went to Dublin and through the influence of a fellow Corkman, found a place in one of the leading Banks. There I remained for five weary years until last summer, when all the Irish banks came out on strike. I hung about for a while, but there was no prospect of an early settlement and presently, with many of my colleagues, I came to London.

I took rooms with a fellow Corkman, Finbar O'Dowd, and at once applied for, and received, Social Security. Soon afterwards, through another fellow Corkman, I got a job in the Islington branch of the Universe and London County Bank. Oh, how I did suffer! If the Dublin bank had cramped my being, this one was hell on earth. The petty niggling spirit of the London people defies description. If you were only half an hour late, they looked down their stupid noses. If you were only a few pounds short at the end of a day, they badgered you without mercy.

After a few experiences of the latter kind, they transferred me from the cashiers to the Inquiry and Information department. Now I sat in a little rabbit-hutch all day, answering letters from clients. These letters were on trivial matters, as important correspondence went to the manager's office, but at least the replies offered me a little scope for self-expression. Here and there I would employ a vivid unusual phrase or add a touch of fancy—once I broke into verse—and it was gratifying to think how the recipients must enjoy them.

But here too, I was up against that narrow, hidebound, English pedantry. Their insistence on trifling details amounted to obsession. Whenever my files were passed for any reason to higher authority, they invariably came back with a carping memorandum: a surname was wrongly spelt, I had dated a letter the year before, there was a nought or so too many on some figure, God help us. There was never a word of praise for my fresh and lively approach. I soon began to see that I was a fish out of water.

I had been in that department a couple of months when I was called one morning to the manager's office. He was a crabby bugger, with a face like a milkman's horse, boney and sad, and a long soft upper lip that moved when he spoke as if he were trying to pick up a lump of sugar. One of my files lay open on the desk before him.

'Ah Cruise,' he said as I came in. No greeting, no remarks about the weather, no asking me to have a chair. A savage, like all of them. 'I must have a word with you about your spelling.'

Spelling, if you don't mind! The piffling complaint of an elderly schoolmaster.

' "I must appologise for the oversight in my last letter",' he read out. 'You have two p's in apologise. And here is "believe", spelt b.e.l.e.i.v.e. I before e, except after c, Cruise. And again: "Perhaps you are not aquainted . . ." You have omitted the c in "acquainted". Elementary mistakes, every one. Do they not teach orthography in Ireland?'

That is another thing I loathe about the English, their eternal gibes at Ireland.

'I don't know why you drag in Ireland, Mr Goodge,' I replied fiercely. I did not call him 'sir'. I call no man 'sir'. 'Chaucer and Shakespeare spelt whatever way they chose.'

'Chaucer and Shakespeare were not employed in this Bank,' he retorted, like the booby he was. Had anyone said that they were? 'A nice impression Miss Butler will get of us.'

Now, although I had never seen her, this same Penelope Butler was a thorn in my flesh. She was a little jumped-up schoolmarm, who had taught in a comprehensive school for less than the Bank was paying me. By the end of the month she was always down to the last penny. And then, bless my soul if she didn't win over half a million in the Football Pools! England was rotten to the core all right when a thing like that could happen. Of course she chucked her job and moved out of our slummy area, and you might think that was the end of her. Not a bit of it! She got drawing facilities at our branch in the new district but left all her business with us, putting on dog, writing in about investments and such. I imagine it soothed her pride, because in the old days when she overdrew by even a couple of pounds the Bank would tick her off, as she had no securities then.

I was so angry to hear the silly old snob prating about her now that I threw discretion to the winds.

'And Miss Butler is such an *important* client!' I said with contempt. 'With all that Football money!'

Mr Goodge looked sharply at me over the rims of his pince-nez.

'I am afraid you are out of your depth in banking, Cruise,' he snapped. 'Our clients are all important to us, and equally so. And we do not refer to matters known to us confidentially, such as where their money derived from. And impertinence cannot be tolerated. You will leave us at the end of your month.'

Out of my depth, in the shallows of the Universe and London County! Impertinence, as if I were a lackey rather than a descendant of the Irish High Kings! If he had been a younger man, I should have demanded satisfaction for those words. As it was, I turned on my heel and marched from the room without deigning to reply.

On several occasions in Dublin our manager there had notified me that my services were no longer required. Then, after some time had elapsed, he would call me back and say that he had reconsidered the matter since. He never made a formal apology, but I felt that one was implied. All that day I waited for a summons from Mr Goodge, and I prepared a little speech to round the incident off in friendly fashion, but nothing happened. He simply was not big enough to own himself in the wrong.

Very well, then, *I* would be magnanimous, *I* would make the overture; and I would be generous enough to agree that there were faults on both sides. But when I asked his secretary to arrange an interview, that she-dragon replied with a sniff that Mr Goodge was not available and declined all further discussion. He actually, it appeared, had meant what he said. I was to be turned away, into the cold, with my wretched monthly pittance, a week before Christmas, when everyone else was making good cheer in honour of the Birth of Our Blessed Lord! The cruelty of the man was sickening, of a piece with England's treatment of our people from time immemorial. Fair play for him, the real culprit was Miss Penelope Butler, who kept on writing those letters to which I was forced to reply. But while this mitigated, it could not excuse, his conduct; and on the day I left I wrote to him, anonymously, telling him just what monumental class of a creep he was.

Now I had to think seriously about the future. I was not too badly off for the moment, having on Finbar's advice, continued to draw the Social Security throughout my spell at the Bank. All the Irish did so, he said : England owed it to us, after the way she had pillaged our country for hundreds of years. But I should register a change of address with the Security crowd, in case they went snooping round and asking questions. His cousin Norah had a flat in the Arabella Road, Kensington, and I could say I was now rooming there. That would take my file out of the Islington area and make things doubly safe. Norah was thoroughly honest and dependable and would tell any snooper that I was out, hunting for work. So that was fixed and it was fine, apart from dashing to Kensington and back in the lunch-hour to draw the money. In hand, I had over four hundred pounds from Security and about half that from the strike fund in Dublin as well as my last month's wage from the Bank. For the present anyhow, I should not starve.

But that was not enough. I wanted to make money, real money, piles of it. A man of my outstanding gifts could not continue all his life as a wage-slave, at the beck and call of creatures like Goodge. It was *contra naturam*, as the Christian Brothers would say. The strike in Ireland was now on the point of settling, and there was an announcement in the Irish press that all who had taken jobs abroad should return at once or their places would be filled. Having taken the plunge and landed here, in this huge city where money flowed like water and my compatriots were making it hand over fist, I could not bear the thought of creeping back to that poor place, that dreary round of work and drink and gossip, where you hardly saw a man you didn't know and everything was always the same, always would be. It is a funny thing about Ireland, her charms are only visible from a long way off. And the work would be killing. In the five months that the Irish banks were closed, apparently, the entire nation had gone on a spree. People bought whatever they wanted and gave cheques for it, since they couldn't be promptly cleared. Humble farmers, small traders, had piled up future overdrafts that would not have disgraced a tycoon. And we should have to sort them all out.

Therefore I decided to burn my boats, stand pat, look about me and use my wits. Irishmen with half my brains were Cabinet Ministers here, trade union leaders, or in local Government, all doing nicely. Of course that was much too dull for the likes of me, I wanted something bold and imaginative, yet lawful. Finbar was always singing the praises of a lad he knew who ran a queer old fiddle on the building sites, something to do with Income Tax vouchers, that pulled in a fortune. I would never stoop to a thing like that, or to any other criminal deed. Oh, I had chances all the same. There was Benedict Geraghty who had been at the Christian Brothers with me in Cork, that I ran across in the Irish club. He was courier for a bunch of counterfeiters in Amsterdam, bringing the notes across to England, and was polluted with the work and the worry. He wanted me as a butty, but I spurned the offer with indignation. It might have landed me in gaol or got me deported, and where was the bonus in that?

The next few months were very hard. All my efforts came to nothing. I tried to break into journalism. Some of the boyos went to blow up the Albert Memorial and only blew up themselves. I wrote a stirring inside account of this affair, with brilliant 'profiles' of the heroic dead and details of their organisation, and took it to a Sunday newspaper, one that was always splashing the IRA. They were all over me in their Features department, it was a wow. But then they called in their Irish 'expert', the hound, who questioned me like a bloody policeman, how did I know this and that, where did I meet the fellows, was there anyone who could corroborate, and the Lord knew what-all. I suppose he was jealous. Anyway, they finished up laughing at me to my face. One of them had the nerve to say I was wasting my gifts, I ought to be writing fiction. As good as called me a liar. But that's the English for you, they'll come straight out with things that decent people keep under their hats.

My savings dwindled fast. I was getting Social Security, but no one could live on that. And the snoopers started annoying Norah, wanted to know what I was doing and why I was always out. They must have been in cahoots with the Labour Exchange as well, because every time I called at her flat there was an impudent communication from it, with details of some ignoble job that I should apply for. My sufferings at this time,

I can tell you, would have melted a heart of stone.

And yet, with it all, one thing never deserted me : the Faith. The holy Faith, that has sustained our people throughout their age-long history of hardship and wrong. Humbly, as a child to his mother, I asked help of Our Lady, Blessed Mary, Mother most amiable, prudent, of all good counsel. I knew she would hear me, would not suffer me to fall by the way. In her own good time, she would stretch forth her hand to bring me relief : secure in the knowledge of that, I faced whatever the future held with serenity.

*

It was in May that a new and terrible blow struck me. I was staying with Norah now, because Finbar had picked a quarrel one night that he was drinking and told me to go. Norah is a decent skin, if ever there was one. She only charged for the room, and very little at that, but she threw in breakfast with it; and if I happened to be knocking about at other meal-times there was always a share for me. And she'd put my wash-ing in with hers, and iron my shirts, and clean my shoes, and send the snoopers about their business. She is the ideal woman, like my own dear mother, God rest and reward her, who brought me breakfast in bed up to the very day that she died.

Norah was great company too, telling jokes and stories and making fun of the English until you'd bust yourself laughing. She knew all the people in the road and they'd tell her things they wouldn't another. One of these was a fellow named Khan, Aziz Akbar Khan, who had the fruit and vegetable shop a few doors away. It was something she heard from him and passed on to me that led to the new disaster.

He had a wife but, a devout Moslem, he was entitled to more and so he invented a second large family at home in Pakistan, to get relief from the Income Tax. This gave me the idea of claiming extra Social Security for a wife in Ireland, in fact, it was strange I didn't think of it sooner. I put in the claim and was expecting the money, with a fat sum of arrears from the day I started drawing; but, by the mean underhand methods such people use, the office found out that I was unmarried and reported it.

I was to be prosecuted, if you don't mind, without I ever drew an extra penny! I had to leave Norah at once, before they nabbed me. She persuaded Khan to take me in until I found new lodgings for myself, and a song and dance he made of it too, telling me how honoured he was and how I should be like his own, his brother. As well he might, for it was all through him that I landed in the ditch; but after a week he presented his 'brother' with a bill for thirty pounds. I all but despaired of humanity, but there was nothing I could do. I was stuck, my Social Security withdrawn, my savings down to a couple of hundred, a hunted, hounded man, faced with crippling new expenses.

*

It was in this darkest of dark moments that help was granted from on high. I was rambling idly through the streets and squares of Kensington, looking sadly into windows at elegant rooms and smiling people, when I came on a palatial building in Norfolk Gardens. A flight of snowy steps led up to the front door, which had a gleaming brass handle, knocker and letter-box on it and a fancy pillar on either side. On one of these pillars was painted the word NORFOLK, on the other, the word HOUSE. It flashed across my mind, after all these months, that this was the address of Penelope Butler, the architect of my ruin. I stood there, thinking bitter thoughts of her, how she'd be writing in for information and advice on matters beyond me, so that sooner or later the file was bound to go to the manager and he would seize on the paltry issue of my orthography. I writhed with shame, recalling that last interview, with all the crushing remarks I thought of later left unspoken, and how, seeking reconciliation in a generous manly way, I had exposed myself to that contemptuous snub.

'Mr Goodge is not available and declines all further discussion.' I seemed to hear those words again, with the snooty English voice and accent, as if I were an office boy, turned out for pinching the office stamps.

And here in this Ritzy house, perhaps at home this very minute, surrounded with comfort, with luxury, lived the woman who was to blame for all!

I had no dream of revenge, no wish to pay her back. Such things are beneath me. But I did consider the very least she could do was to make restitution. Should I not write to her, describing the pass to which she had brought me and frankly asking for help? Or better, should I not call on her and do so? Letters are cold and stiff and I am not at my best in them, whereas I have a way with women that is all but irresistible. My looks, beautiful rather than handsome with the fine Irish eyes, long lashes and curly hair, but redeemed from all effeminacy by the firm nose and mouth and strongly moulded chin: the ease and grace of manner: the lithe athletic frame: the soft caressing Irish voice; and that cajoling warmth of expression, call it blarney if you will, that topples every woman, be she never so frigid. All these assets were mine, waiting to serve me and save me and counting them over all at once I saw with blinding clarity the way out of my troubles.

I would marry Penelope Butler and make her fortune mine.

Why not? True, I had never seen her, and the mental picture I had formed from her correspondence was not prepossessing. A schoolmarm of forty or so, a dried-up spinster, with a flat chest and mousy hair, and a snoozing cat on her knee while she wrote her blasted letters, was what I imagined. But you cannot expect to have all you want in this vale of tears. You learn to take the rough with the smooth. There was Paddy Flynn in Cork now, whose wife could nearly be his mother, with diabetes and as sour as a pickled onion—when he got hitched up with her, everyone said he was mad. But after they were married three months, didn't the uncle die and she fall in for twenty thousand pounds, to balance it out? And all in all they are as contented as most married people I know. They don't speak to each other, haven't spoken for years, but they manage to rub along.

So I too was prepared to overlook the deficiencies of Penelope Butler for the sake of her real attractions. The next step now was to plan my courtship of her, and a delicate business it would be. I must, to begin with, find a pretext for getting in touch with her, solid grounds for a meeting with nothing contrived about it, or she would smell a rat. Once that hurdle was left behind, my personality would do the rest and I had no fears of the outcome.

As I stood there, deep in meditation, my eye fell on a notice board in the basement window announcing a vacancy in the house. A top flat was for letting, and I saw immediately that here was my chance. As a fellow tenant I could be running across Penelope all the time, in the lift, on the stairs, walking about the private garden. I would show little kindnesses to her, such as women love, bring her flowers, run her errands, and win her over before she knew it. It would take a shocking amount of money, but so did Aziz Akbar Khan, without the prospect there of any return for the outlay.

Now I went up the steps and studied the row of doorbells, each with a name to it only for Top Floor 2, which was blank. Top Floor 1 was Miss P. Butler. It seemed like a wink from heaven: we should be not merely under the one roof but next-door neighbours too. I hurried down to the basement and rang the bell, informing the crusty old fellow who answered that I proposed to rent the vacant flat. He wasn't taken with me at all, that much stuck out. If I had asked him to buy a sewing-machine, he couldn't have made me less welcome. After looking me over in a suspicious kind of way, he growled: 'Ho, do you? You must see the Agent. I'm the caretaker,' and shut the door in my face.

The Agent's address was on the board. He lived some distance off and, when I had run him to earth, he was for making difficulties too. He wanted me to view the premises before I took them and, when I said it wasn't necessary, he told me it was always done. In England, by the way, you always have to do what is always done.

'The flat may not be to your liking,' he said, doubtfully. He was a little worried man, the type that sees trouble round every corner.

'Let me take care of that,' I said, switching on the charm. 'I'm after landing here from across the water, with nowhere to lay my poor head.'

'Then you require immediate possession?' he asked, with a frightened air. 'This is most unusual.'

Oh dear me, the carry-on then! You'd think it was Buckingham Palace. He gave me their standard agreement to look at, and you'd never believe what was in it, clause after clause. Flat for personal and private use only, no commercial undertaking to be carried on there, no sub-letting, no lodgers or paying guests, no coloured people, no livestock other than one pet dog or cat, no this, that or the other. And he wanted references! a banker's and a personal, and a whole lot of details about myself that didn't concern him. He seemed to be doing his level best to put me off. But I argued him to a finish and the end of it was, I could have immediate possession on paying a month's rent down. In this period he would take my references up and, if satisfactory, prepare a formal Agreement for my signature.

So that was that. I gave him a cheque for a hundred and fifty pounds, which all but left me high and dry, and he gave me the keys and the application form to fill out. 'On the understanding that you let me have it, completed, before you move in,' said the dope, in his flustered way. 'This is all quite irregular. I have known nothing like it before.'

Now here was another headache! What should I do for references? It was too bad I had fallen out with Finbar, he was the one for teasers like that. From the cut of the Agent's jib, I could guess he'd be none too happy with Norah or Aziz Akbar Khan, and most other people I knew had no fixed address. There was a decent fellow Corkman at the Universe and London County that I'd kept up with, Brendan McCarthy, but he was under notice now. The Agent might start checking on him. But thinking of Brendan, I got a brainwave. I rang him up and asked if any of the senior staff were on holidays. By the mercy of God, old Goodge himself had just gone away for a month, and I could give his name as both banking and personal referee. I would instruct the Agent to mark the letter *Personal*: *to wait*—lest that she-devil typist ran off with it to the Deputy—explaining that Goodge was away at present. That would give me a breather, anyhow. Much can happen in a month, and there's no sense crossing a bridge until you come to it.

Everything now had fallen wonderfully into place. I filled out the application at once, in the Post Office Arabella Road, and mailed it Express. Mr. Brooke should see I was a man of my word. Then I went back to the fruit shop and broke the news of my departure to Khan. Amiable as ever, he told me while it grieved him his 'brother' should go it was all for the best. For some peculiar Moslem reason, the whole house was shortly to be purified and there would have been no room while this was going on.

I started moving into Norfolk House next day. Norah lent me a camp bed, blankets and linen, a couple of chairs, china and cutlery, a kettle and frypan, a record-player and a statue of the Sacred Heart. And she gave me bread, butter, eggs, tea, sugar, and a packet of smokes, God bless and reward her. It was the first Wednesday in June and there was an Irish horse running in the Derby, an outsider at 35 to 1, called Nothing Venture; and when I saw that I clapped on a couple of quid, the sagacious beast came romping home, and there was £70 to help me set up house.

I am far from superstitious but, as I saw it, that was an omen of more good luck on the way. It must be, the Powers above were watching over my destiny. I now prepared to rush the citadel next door and to carry off the prize.

Two

By this time, the imaginary face and figure of the woman were so real to me that I could have drawn them to the life. When she opened her door in reply to my knock, her appearance came as a total surprise. And as a relief. Marriage to that one, after all, would be no penance. She was young and pretty, and she was my type. You can keep the redheads and raven beauties, which are two a penny at home, if I can have a Saxon blonde, with hair like a field of ripening corn, eyes like pools reflecting the sky, skin like a magnolia petal, the faintest rosy tinge in either cheek, no more. And she had class. It was in her ankles and wrists and the way she carried herself. Irishwomen mostly walk as if they were carrying a pail or else in pup. She had a light springing elastic tread and moved like a greyhound.

I was frankly bowled over, unable to do what was needed and quickly adjust my plan of campaign. This was, to break the ice by inquiring if she had seen my cat. It was to have led to a discussion of cats on familiar lines, of their ways and peculiarities, their wisdom, their beauty, their superiority over the dog, indeed over most humans, and the anxiety their owners must feel if they went astray. The Miss Butler of my supposing would have risen to this like a trout to a fly. I should have been off and running. But the real one had no interest in cats whatever. She asked in a perfunctory way what my cat was like and then denied having seen one of his description; and, what was worse, she plainly expected that now I would go.

I had to think and act swiftly. I decided the moment had come for a liberal display of charm. Boldly passing her by as she stood in the door, I began to explore her flat, showing an interest in this, admiring that, complimenting her on her taste and generally buttering her up. In all sincerity, too, the place was a fairyland. It was twin to the one next door and when I thought of my rooms, bare, bleak, comfortless, and saw what she had made of hers, with soft carpets and lovely curtains, elegant tables and comfortable chairs, silver flowerbowls and boxes, my heart was heavy at the world's injustice. None of that, of course, appeared in my manner. Never let anyone see into your mind, is a favourite maxim of my father's and he keeps to it well, except when he takes a jar too many and whatever happens to be in *his* mind then comes spilling out of its own accord.

I smiled upon her, talked easily and well, sparkled in fact, caressed her with eyes and voice. None of it had any effect at all. She was barely human. There was I, a guest, a visitor, a stranger, and instead of making me welcome and asking about myself as we do with strangers at home, she took no interest whatever. When I offered a penny for her thoughts, she replied: 'I was wondering, frankly, to what I owe this visit'! And the way she said it! not crossly or scornfully, but in a cool offhand tone as if it didn't really matter. Common English people talk down to you, deliberately putting on airs; but the classy ones can make you feel inferior much more successfully, just by being their natural selves.

Then I told her I wanted a drink. She ought to have realised that herself and I expected her to apologise for not having done so. But, bless my soul, all she said was, 'Then perhaps you had better go to a public-house.' I never heard anything so barbarous in all my life. There was a whole great army of bottles and cutglass decanters on a side-table in the room, and she would not even take the few little steps across to them, and pour a drink for me.

I lost my patience then, and determined to shake her out of her cool. That is a thing I'm really good at, when anyone needs it. The secret of the game is, surprise. In the calmest way in the world, you come up with something they never thought to hear, and that you've just invented. There was this Customs man at Holyhead when I came over, high-hatting me about the whisky I didn't declare, on and on, the supercilious bugger. At last I said wearily, 'Okay, what's this I owe you? I can't stand here all day, arguing with an Arab.' He was a Jew. 'Arab! Arab! Arab!' yells he, 'Who are you calling an Arab?' 'Are you not one?' says I, looking him over, kind of puzzled. 'You're the spit and image of a lad I knew at Port Said.' Oh, I bounced him nicely.

So, applying this technique, I drew a bow at a venture on your woman. To begin with, I asked why she was so stand-offish when the other tenants were so free and easy. I had caught a few glimpses of those same tenants, and a snootier crowd of buttoned-up toffee-noses you needn't hope to find. She came back at me, giving me to understand that, on the contrary, they kept themselves to themselves as gentlemen should. They might do with her, I said—this was the pay off—because she was considered a dark horse. I guessed that would rock her and it did. I pointed out that she had moved in here from a dump in Camden Town—I knew that from records at the Bank, but she would think the tenants were chatting about it— and was living it up without an occupation or visible means of support.

Oh, I laid it on, and gave myself up to the pleasure of it, but afterwards I saw that it was an error of judgement. I had let her needle me into a course which could jeopardise my whole campaign. The idea was, by arousing her fears, to bring her round to me, looking for comfort and reassurance; but it misfired altogether. In fact, she turned quite nasty and all but threw me out. I put things right again, of course, with a friendly tactful note that I dropped through her letterbox that evening. And to some extent, I now had the length of her foot, something to guide me a little in future. The next time we met it would not be as strangers, and I would try a completely different approach. What it would be, I could not foretell. I must wait for circumstances to unfold and a situation to develop, and improvise according to them.

*

For a good long time there seemed to be no way. Communication between the two of us was halted. She never answered my note, which shocked me in one of her breeding. I was chary of dropping in again until there was a powerful reason for it. My charm alone was not enough, because she was too wrapped up in herself to notice it. Most women, meeting me for the first time, look me over with immediate interest and approval, take me in, admire my appearance, and are well-disposed from the start. This one, I will bet, had not the faintest idea of what I was like, the colour of my hair and eyes, the timbre of my voice, the clothes I had on me. She merely saw me as an unwelcome interruption, without any specific qualities.

And the days were flitting by, bringing nearer the return of Mr Goodge and my inevitable exposure. By then, if things had gone smoothly, I should have been well on the way to getting myself engaged. I might even with luck, when Mr Brooke turned me away, have moved into Penelope's flat. But here I was, with everything still to do, my money dwindling fast and no prospect of more coming in.

The strange part was that, for all we lived cheek by jowl, I never ran into her, never got the chance of carrying her parcels or even of opening a door for her, nothing. It must be, she went in and out like a mouse for I never heard her. One day I caught sight of her in the garden, sitting under a tree, reading a book, pretty as paint. I hurried into the garden myself and paced to and fro like a sentry, near her, humming the Londonderry Air, and she never once looked up. Utterly self-absorbed. Then a bloody little dog that was trotting about came over and sniffed at my ankle. Much as I loathe all dogs, I stooped to pat this one, hoping it might be hers. A sure way to win the hearts of the English is to make a fuss of their wretched dogs.

'And aren't you the great little man,' I was cooing. 'Aren't you the grand little fellow!'

With that, he bit me severely on the thumb, and a frightful old witch called from a window, I was to leave Benjy alone, he didn't like strangers. 'You could apologise, ma'am, all the same,' I shouted back. The blood was streaming. 'Leave Benjy alone and he'll do you no harm,' the beldame hollered. 'It was entirely your fault, I saw you.'

All this happened within a few yards of Penelope Butler and, would you believe it, she never stopped reading then.

One other day, it seemed I was getting a break at last. I was strolling through the Park, near that sandy road where the swells of London go riding. And didn't your woman come cantering down it, sitting nicely into the saddle too, hands and heels well down, and on a mare that would have cost her three, maybe four, hundred pounds. She never saw me, of course, I was the Invisible Man. She cantered off to the end of the track and turned in my direction again. Just then, from the opposite way, came a kid on a pony, in trouble, clutching the withers, feet out of stirrups, bum in the air, bawling oh oh oh!

Here was the moment. Without hesitation, regardless of my personal safety, I flew to the rescue. The blood of my gallant race permitted no less. I grabbed the bridle as the pony shot by and with mingled courage and skill brought the creature up standing. The hoofbeats of Penelope's mare were growing louder but I never turned my head, just went on with soothing the kid, gentle and soft as a mother. I really thought I had it made, for where's the woman of any race that could ever resist a hero? She'd rein in now, congratulate me, say it was the finest thing she ever saw, and it was well I chanced to be there. But, the devil take her, she cantered easily past, looking straight ahead, thinking only of herself as usual, with never an eye to spare for anyone else. And now the riding-mistress caught up with us and without taking the least notice of me, no more than if I was a log of wood, began to scold: 'Gerard, how often must I tell you, if your mount runs away, to lean back and pull?'

God Almighty, these English get me to the fair. Not a word of thanks or was I all right. And I gained nothing by it, not a thing in the world. That's the last time I'll save any life over here. There's no sense in gallant deeds unless somebody marks them up to you.

I was despondent for days after that, thinking I really was scuppered now. For the first time I wondered if heaven were on my side after all. And then, suddenly, all was changed by a kind of miracle. Help came from a quarter where I looked for it least, and in the most improbable way. The wheels of Fate were set in motion by Aziz Akbar Khan.

✻

He got them moving with an invitation to dinner. I was astounded, for he was a man of close and careful habits and never entertained a soul, that I knew. All the time I was there I never had bite or sup, except one roasting day when the Begum brought me a pot of jasmine tea, icy cold and delicious. She put it down before me with a motherly smile, and I was really touched; but it figured in the weekly bill to the tune of 75p. Now here was a note asking me to a full dinner at nine o'clock on the following day!

When I reached his house, there was a further surprise. Khan was a pious Moslem, who never took a drink or allowed it under his roof. Today, in the private sanctum where we would chat together until the meal was ready, there was a bottle of Scotch on the table, a siphon and a single glass. He poured me a generous tot, all but Irish in scale, and politely regretted that he could not join me. It was great Scotch too, the best, he evidently knew his way about.

Khan was an amusing fellow, a real card. With the customers, or in any dealings with English people, he talked a kind of pidgin, of limited vocabulary and almost no grammar.

With me and Norah and such, he spoke a fluent racy English, having in his younger days studied at Calcutta and narrowly failed to get a degree. The beauty of pidgin was, he averred, that it prevented serious discussion, whether of his prices, the quality of his goods or mistakes in a reckoning. Customers would try to get their points across but after a while gave up in despair. With officials also, taxmen, inspectors and the like, he followed the same fruitful policy, and was widely known among them as a man better left in peace.

'Well now, dear boy, tell me what you've been up to,' he began, sipping some hellish herbal brew. 'Long time no see. What do you think of your new abode? Very very fine it did look to me, when I delivered my little note. Almost I was afraid to mount those immaculate steps.'

He had a warm sympathetic way of talking, just like the people at home, that made you feel your concerns were his and drew you out. I told him about the flat and the fine big rooms I had, with the grand views over London and the private garden and the classy tenants, pushing it a little, wanting to make an impression. He listened, smiling, with his head on one side, looking at me with the affectionate air he always had. From time to time he topped up my glass, without stint, as if his abhorrence of liquor were just a foolish caprice on his part and did not apply to others. My tongue freely wagging, I went on about Penelope, her gorgeous flat, the mare she rode in the Park and her lovely face, although my intention had been to leave her out of it, because Khan always disparaged white women, even Norah. 'Their hands are too big,' he would say, 'and their breasts are too small.' His ideal was the Begum, as broad as she was long, with a bosom like two great melons and tiny paws like a mole : every woman he saw, he measured against her, and found them wanting. But this evening he let my raptures pass. He smiled away and nodded his understanding, as if carried along by, and sharing, my enthusiasm.

'So then a brilliant new style, brilliant new friends, brilliant new life,' he said, topping me up. Then with gentle pathos,

'There will be no time in future to spare for your brother Khan.'

I repudiated the charge with tipsy warmth. 'How can you say so?' I cried. 'Making new friends doesn't mean discarding the old. I never threw one of them over in my life.'

This was the holy truth. In the matter of personal relations my past was strewn with wreckage, but only because, in my frank guileless way, I was apt to believe that people were friends when, like Finbar O'Dowd, they ultimately turned out to be snakes in the grass.

My brother Khan was immensely cheered by these words. 'I did not doubt it seriously,' he said. 'And I know you will wish to help your brother in a little problem he has.'

He proceeded to lay the little problem bare. The impending purification, for Moslem reasons, of his dwelling called for its evacuation by the family, to allow the Imam and his assistants a free hand. Where should the family go? Hotels were ruinous in London, and not always kind to people from over the sea. It was a matter of a day or two, no more. If they could move in perhaps with their brother? They would be no trouble, for they would bring their own bedding and food. Indeed, they might prove a comfort. The Begum would cook him many fine dishes. It was not a thing he would propose to everyone but the Irish, he knew, had as exalted an idea of hospitality and the claim upon it as the followers of the Prophet had themselves.

Now at last, too late, I understood the purpose of the invitation to dinner. 'Well, I hardly know what to say,' I demurred, playing for time. 'There's plenty of room for one, all right. I'm not too sure about ten.'

'Oh, our people fold into very small space, we are accustomed to that,' he assured me. 'There were twenty-seven in my father's house, half the size of this.'

'And Norfolk House has a hundred and one stupid rules about who comes in,' I hurried on. I could not bring myself to mention that cruel imperialist embargo on colour. 'No lodgers, no paying guests . . .'

'Then I must not think of paying you, must I?' he cried eagerly, as if anxious to comply with every requirement. 'And we are quiet people. No one shall know we are there.'

A piercing howl from one of the children upstairs seemed to contradict him. I kept up the arguments and excuses, which he parried softly and urbanely, ruthless as a spider and persistent as a fly. The cooking noises in the kitchen ceased and I waited for the Begum's head to look round the door, announcing in her silent way that dinner was served. Nothing happened, however, and Khan continued at intervals to freshen my glass. He must have arranged with his wife to hold things back until I threw in the sponge.

Now something occurred which often does with me when I am drinking. In the twinkling of an eye, as fast as you'd flip a coin, I switched to a different, opposite, point of view. Time and again I have ended an evening arguing vociferously against all I said earlier on. This power of seeing both sides of a question, no doubt, was what Shaw meant by 'the flexibility of the Irish mind'. It always foxes the English, whose thoughts —if that is the word—plod slowly along in a groove. All at once the idea of installing the Khans in Norfolk House presented itself as an excellent one. It would be thumbing my nose at the whole snooty bunch of them there. Unknown to them, but under their very noses, would be a group of despised downtrodden coloured people, oppressed and exploited by their like for centuries, just as mine were. The thought of their rage if they ever found out was something to feast on. Miss Penelope Butler would feel herself contaminated by their very presence. What the devil got in me at all, that I was cracking her up to Khan only half an hour since? The woman who lost me my job, treated me like dirt when I paid her a neighbourly call, whom I was prepared to marry and who, when I wanted a drink, coldly replied, 'Then go to some sleazy pub, where you belong'!

'I'll do it!' I shouted, furious at the memory. 'A small revenge for Amritsar!'

125

Khan lovingly poured the heel of the Scotch into my glass. 'It is my brother's true voice that I am hearing now,' he said. 'But why Amritsar? How does Amritsar come into the situation?'

'An English atrocity!' I cried, fiercely banging the table. 'A bloody massacre of your people!'

'They were not our people, they were of the Punjab,' said Khan. 'And it was an Irish regiment killing them. We have always loved Ireland for it.'

'Sure, there's nothing we wouldn't do for you!' I assured him, quick as a flash, the flexible mind to the fore again.

'Shall we say, then, tomorrow?'

'Tomorrow it is. But come after dark.'

That was my happiest evening for a very long time. The meal was on the frugal side, a vegetable curry with rice, and some bruised mangoes to follow. But better a dinner of herbs where love is, and all that jazz. I sang 'The Wearing of the Green', 'The Wexford Boys' and 'Who Fears to Speak', winding up with 'Galway Bay'. Khan said with a voice like mine I ought to be earning a fortune. I said how much it would mean to me, would add to my pleasure in life, having them all round my hearth; and soon after that I went home.

＊

It must be, there was something in that curry that disagreed with me. Next morning I woke up feeling desperate. My head was fit to burst, my tongue was ashy, yellow and purple spots were swarming in front of my eyes. I realised bitterly, too, that I had been conned. I did not want to house that wretched family, don't mind if it was only a day or two. Wily Khan had taken advantage of my goodness to impose himself on me. It is my great drawback to be no match for people like that.

I half determined to put him off. In fact, I was cudgelling my brains for a plausible excuse when the telephone rang and there was McCarthy, with the heartwarming news that Mr Goodge was delayed. The silly old fool was watching birds in

Devon and tumbled over a cliff. I saw that my luck was in again, and decided to let the Khans come after all. Thank heaven I did! and how strange is life, with small chance happenings leading to great events.

As I had stipulated, the family arrived after dark and nobody saw them. They had a shocking amount of gear, food and cooking utensils and pallets to sleep on, done up in paper and string. I crammed it all into the goods lift while Mrs Khan and the children squeezed into the passenger. Khan refused to go in lifts because they were always collapsing in Pakistan. He placidly saw his spouse and offspring off, however, and then followed by means of the fire escape. It was after midnight when I got them and their chattels all safely bestowed in the flat and Mrs Khan, having prepared a herbal brew for Khan, took herself and the children to bed. They dossed down on the floor of one room, nestling against each other like bunnies in a warren and, as Khan had promised, folding into very small space. Khan said he would talk to his brother while he drank his tea.

'And the beautiful lady next door?' he began. 'Am I to see her?'

'I hope not,' said I. 'You are not supposed to be here, and she's one that would start complaining.'

'That would not be too kind at all,' said Khan, sadly. 'Yesterday, you made her sound a jolly decent young girl.'

'And isn't she English? You know what pigheads they are about rules.'

'Indeed, yes, it is so.' Khan sighed, pensively stirring the brew. 'They glory in the making of rules, for themselves and for others. They live by rules. That is an odd thing about them, for they are not in general a stupid people.'

'Would you say that? I think they are as stupid as can be.'

'No, no,' murmured Khan. 'Excuse me, this is hatred speaking. Those who think them stupid live to find out their mistake. The lady is rich, you said.'

'Stinking.'

127

'I do not understand this expression, "stinking rich",' Khan declared with a frown. 'Riches can never stink. But let us consider the lady and her rules. She is not to know we are here, you say. But why? Then she will not know that the rules are broken. Poor girl, she will have no chance to put things right.'

'Right, is it, her complaining and you being told to get out, and me as well, most likely.'

'It does not follow that this would happen,' said Khan. 'The English are very soft-hearted people. They love to come to the rescue at any time, and when there is no reason why they should they cannot resist it. If we had famine or earthquake at home, eagerly eagerly they poured their money out. An uncle of mine was employed to administer such a Relief Fund once. He was able to build a luxury hotel.'

At the recollection of this, his round sallow face lit up with a curious inner radiance, like a lantern or the rising moon. He shut his eyes and dropped his head on his breast, deep in thought. Once or twice I began to speak, but he held up an authoritative little paw for silence. He communed thus with himself for a while, lips gently moving as if in prayer, features still aglow; and then, without opening his eyes, in a far-away dreamy voice, he shared with me the fruits of his meditation.

'Yess! Yess! We are most unfortunate people, indeed we are most wretched. We are newly come to a foreign land and everyone takes advantage of our ignorance. We have found a dwelling place, we are on the brink of moving in. But then the robber landlord, the robber Hindu, what does he say? That he must have money, much money, over and above the rent, cash down, bang. I tell him, This highly illegal, he says, That is too bad. We are in despair, we are sitting among our traps on the road. Then Allah in his mercy sends you walking by. You stop short, you gasp, you inquire, your good Irish heart throbs with compassion at this hard-luck story. You take us in, friendless, forlorn, as we are. Still we wish for a home and not to be a burden to you. But the money, from where will come the money to satisfy this crocodile Hindu? For without it, here we must remain. That,' concluded Khan briskly, raising his head and opening his eyes, 'is the scenario. It is up to you to put it over.'

I was feeling giddy now, used as I was to the sluggish pace of the English mind.

'I am to tell Miss Butler all that? And you really suppose she'd swallow it? I thought you said the English weren't stupid.'

'Nor are they, but they will believe anything if they want to. Little foreign children without a roof, father powerless to help them, that is right down the English street. And, my brother,' said Khan, suddenly grave, 'it is killing two birds with one stone. There will be a nice little nest-egg for you, to repay your kindness to me. For I shall be content with but a half of the money. I shall not dream of taking more. That would not be right.' He beamed at me, his dark plummy eyes all moist with affection.

The divil take it, one could but try. Here was a valid excuse to approach Miss Butler again. I had nothing to lose. In fact, I had much to gain, by showing myself in a new and attractive light. So far, she had only seen me as the assured sophisticated man of the world, witty and charming. Now she would discover my heart of gold, my concern for my fellow beings, my warm response to those in trouble.

'How—?'

'As much as possible,' said Khan. 'But prudence, prudence. Be careful not to exaggerate. Before the eye of my mind there leaps the figure of a hundred pounds. It could be more, I hope not less. I must leave this to you, as the man on the spot. Feel your way, feel your way.'

I had one last little scruple. 'But it must never come out,' I warned him. 'I'm sure you'll agree, the fewer the people that know, the better. Are you proposing to tell Mrs Khan?'

'Not on your Nelly,' her lord replied with a wink.

And so the die was cast.

Three

The next part of my story is harrowing beyond words. To look back on, I mean, in the light of what came after. For everything went so wonderfully well and the sun had apparently broken through the clouds at last. For a time, a cruelly short one, I was the happiest man in the world.

Reader, I fell in love. You have heard that I was willing to marry Miss Butler, no matter how old or plain she might be, and that when I found her young and lovely I was quite bowled over. But that was the artist in me, responding to beauty. My heart was untouched. If anything, I felt hostile, on account of her snooty manner and her callous behaviour over that drink. But, even as I showed her a new facet of my coruscating personality, so did she reveal, or appear to reveal, one of hers. She displayed, or seemed to, a womanly kindness that made her worthy to stand with my mother, God rest her, and Norah Kilbane.

I called on her the evening after the Khans arrived. It had been a difficult day. The children were fretful, squabbling and crying until even the imperturbable Aziz lost patience and started to bawl. Mrs Khan was at loggerheads with the kitchen stove. The stench of curry was overpowering and never cleared away. I bought an Indian record to calm them down but it was Hindu temple music and only made them shriek the louder.

The pretext for my call was that a baby in my flat was cold, and had Miss Butler a shawl to lend us? In the stiff cutting way she has, she pointed out that the weather was piping hot. But sure enough, as Khan had predicted, on hearing that the family was from Pakistan, miserable in our northern climate, she came round. She gave me a beautiful shawl, of a blue to match her eyes and light as a feather, I never knew anything like it. My mother always had a shawl on her, summer and winter, but hers used to weigh pounds and pounds. Khan cheered up no end when he saw it and gave it at once to his wife, as a sweetener.

Later I called again, as I had promised, to explain the whole position, and this time everything went with a bang. Either I was inspired or the Blessed Virgin put the words in my mouth, but I never once went wrong. I piled it on like a hero, how the family had been squatting dismally on the pavement outside the flat they had rented, because the owner wouldn't let them in without a deposit of eight hundred pounds. That was a stroke of genius, the figure just tripped off my tongue, I had intended to say, one hundred. They had no money, no work, no friends, they were desperate.

Penelope was touched, I could see, but she wanted to know why I should get myself involved; and so I treated her to some of the highminded crap that English people can never resist.

'Was I to pass them by on the other side of the road?' I asked her pathetically. 'We are all involved in each other, from the moment that we are born. And where is the meaning in life, if we only think of ourselves?'

That class of bilge. Oh, it worked like a charm, it got her. By now she was giving me drinks, one after the other. But, as Khan had advised, I was not going to push it. I asked her for nothing, never so much as hinted, merely said that somehow I must raise the money, having only a hundred pounds to spare myself. And she believed it, every single word. She made objections, spoke of bodies that were there to help the immigrants, but never questioned the facts. It was like diddling a baby.

'And you still make out, they are not a stupid nation?' I inquired of Khan, when I had finished telling him this, or as much as he ought to know.

'I do,' he replied. 'English persons of her class invariably

speak the truth themselves—it is another of their oddities—
and assume that others will do the same. But if they find them
out, there are no second chances. It makes life extremely dull,
but I do not call it stupid.'

Now I had to lie doggo awhile, supposedly running here and
there and putting the bite on my wealthy friends. The stink of
curry grew steadily worse, each successive meal adding a quota
to what already poisoned the air, in grisly accumulation. Then
one evening my outside doorbell started to ring and I sensed
that someone was on the warpath. There was a shocking din
in the flat, with the baby howling and Khan putting the older
boys through the Koran, he reading a verse and they chanting
it after him at the top of their lungs. He was none too pleased
at the interruption, as he took religious matters very seriously,
but he left off when I asked him and Mrs Khan stifled the
baby's voice in her vast bosom. Soon we were all as quiet as
mice and waited, scarcely breathing, for the bell to stop.

It rang again and again, as if to say, Come on out, I know
you are there. I reckoned it must be Mr Brooke, these mild
scared little men are devils for obstinacy. At last he gave up,
however, and there was peace for a time. I was just inside the
door, listening for all I was worth, but the construction here is
so solid I heard nothing, only the lift coming up and somebody
getting out on our floor. Presently it went down again, and
there was another interval of peace, after which came a gentle
knock on my door.

It was Penelope! Making her first-ever approach to me.
She was looking flustered, even a little guilty, but her manner
was cordial and she agreed at once to our moving into her flat
for a quiet talk. As I thought, Mr Brooke had been at her. The
tenants, selfish bastards, were complaining of the smell and of
the noise, although this was only the second time there was
anything like a real uproar.

She had fobbed him off. She hadn't betrayed me. She was
staunch. My heart began to sing in my breast. Now I really
went to town, telling the tale in the grand manner, how I had

drawn blank after blank among the hard-hearted rich, surrounded with luxury as they were, indifferent to the woes of mankind. I was amazed at my own eloquence. On and on it poured out, working steadily up to the climax at which I intended to ask her, could she perhaps make some contribution, even a hundred pounds, as I was going to do myself.

And, just as I was getting there, she suddenly offered to advance the whole amount! Calm and matter-of-fact, without any flourish or drama, simple, direct, in the English way. Yes, the English way. That was how I thought of it then. All my hatred of this people disappeared in the twinkling of an eye. At that moment I thought them superior to everyone else in the world. My rancours against them, I realised, had been due to a secret grudging sense of their greater worth, and to avow it frankly at last was a kind of liberation for me.

As for Penelope herself, I fell head over heels in love with her, then and there. I can't even remember just what I said, except that I asked for some whisky. I fairly babbled with bliss. She actually, the angel, blamed herself for not having thought of it sooner! Cool and business-like as ever, she promised to go to her Bank first thing in the morning and fetch the money. Hardly knowing if I were on my head or my heels, I told her I must break the wonderful news to the Khans without delay. We fixed an appointment for the morrow and off I went.

'I think my brother's patience has been rewarded,' smiled Khan, as I came in, treading on air. 'It is well. My little home is ready now. I need not trespass on him further. And the brass tacks, how many?'

Even in that dizzy moment I kept my common sense.

'A hundred, as you suggested.'

'No more? Ai! But all is as Allah wishes.' He delivered himself of a speech in his own tongue, a quote from the Koran most likely. 'I had thought the curry would have done its work better, but perhaps she enjoyed it.'

*

I lay awake for hours that night, thinking of Penelope, her queenly face and figure, her voice, her clothes, her bank balance. Then I fell asleep and dreamed of her, the one dream over and over again, how I asked for a loan of sheets and she went to a cupboard for them, only there were no sheets in it, just money, piles and piles on every shelf. She gave me an armful of notes and told me, be sure and air them well before they were used. At this time I was forever dreaming of money, winning it somehow, or getting a fat legacy, or finding a large amount somewhere, carelessly left behind by the owner; and in that very same joyful moment waking up to the bitter fact of my penury. The shock was always so cruel, I dreaded falling asleep. Now, there was nothing to fear, no terrible sinking of the heart as I opened my eyes; the reality was even more blessed than the dream.

She was to hand over the money at eleven in the morning, and I was there on the dot with a strong leather bag that I'd borrowed from the Universe and London County. Then something rather unfortunate happened. The sight of all those crisp clean notes must have carried me away, for without stopping to think I mechanically told them over at speed, for all the world as if I were still at the Bank and she making a deposit! They were tenners, eighty of them, and I rustled my way through the lot as only an experienced teller could. The count was finished before I realised what I had done. It was the kind of lapse that might have led to trouble with a more alert or suspicious person. Luckily, she was too much the lady to be observant or analytical but it was a narrow squeak. I should never make a criminal, that is for sure.

Our business concluded, I returned to the flat, where Khan was hovering in the hallway. He licked his lips at the sight of the bag and made to follow me into my room, but I hurriedly shut the door. Having taken out his fifty pounds, and fifty for myself, I locked the bag again and hid it under the bed. For greater security, I locked the door of my room after leaving it too. Khan was waiting just outside with a dreamy look on his face.

'My brother is a careful man,' he said softly, 'and he is right to be so. There are many bad characters in the world, many bad things take place all around us.'

'Here is your share,' I said, and gave him the money.

'My share,' Khan echoed tonelessly, as if he hadn't an idea what this could mean.

'Of the hundred. Didn't we agree to split fifty-fifty?'

'Yes, we agreed on *fifty-fifty*,' said Khan with emphasis, studying the notes in a dubious kind of way. 'And, between gentleman, an agreement is a sacred thing.'

I resented that very much. What reason had he to doubt my word? I think the trouble with Orientals is, their own minds work in such peculiar labyrinthian coils that simple direct dealing is apt to fox them. He had suggested the amount himself, and claimed the half of it, which was cool enough at that. It had been his idea, all right, but who was it carried it through? He couldn't have done it, he would never have got a toe in Penelope's door. And the seven hundred extra were a bonanza due to my quick thinking and artistry, in which he had no hand at all.

But I let it pass without comment, being in a hurry to get away. I had promised Norah to bring her out to lunch, the very least I could do after all her kindness, now that my ship was in. Time was moving on and you had to get to Wimpy's early, if you wanted a table to yourself. Now I ran back to Penelope and persuaded her to manage the exodus of the mother and kids. I told her that Mrs K. was scared of the lift and that I must go ahead and find a taxi. She was far from delighted, but she agreed and, having introduced the family to her, I took my hook. That about finding a taxi was correct, only it was for me, not the Khans. I reckoned that once they were out of the house they could shift for themselves, especially as Khan was having a fit of sulks. He seemed to think he had been outsmarted, which he wasn't used to at all.

Norah was ready, all dolled up and with a good deal of rouge on her face. She might have a heart of gold but when she put her finery on she looked like a tramp from the quays. Her make-up broke off suddenly at the line of her jaw, as if it were a mask, and the neck beneath it could have done with soap and water. Her finger-nails were grimy, too, I wouldn't have wished for Penelope to see us together.

She was not herself today, what was more. One of the grand things about her was that she always agreed to whatever you might be suggesting. She made a man feel that he knew best and that every decision could safely be left to him. She lived in a continual state of applause. But now, when I said we must hurry on to Wimpy's without delay, she pulled a face and told me Wimpy's was not her idea of a treat. There had been nothing said about treats, all I did was ask her to lunch. I said nothing as to the wherefore, beyond that I'd had a wee piece of luck. She'd have laughed herself silly over the truth, but no good ever comes of telling the whole of a story, except you made it up for a business reason.

'I wish now, we'd go to Santorelli,' says she, as cool as be damned. 'Will you not bring me there?'

If you don't mind! Santorelli was a slap-up joint with waiters and a barbecue, and bunches of plastic grapes hung from the ceiling, like it was Italy. We'd never get away out of that under a couple of pounds apiece. There is a touch of the gold-digger in even the best of women. *Noblesse oblige*, however, and to Santorelli we went. Fair play for Norah, she took a dish of spaghetti and one glass of wine, so that part of it wasn't too fierce after all; but the food was hardly on the table before she was throwing out hints about some film at the Odeon.

It was sad all right to see her behaving so much out of character, it clouded her image for me. This wasn't the Norah I knew, with the ready smile and the cheery crack, mending, washing, ironing, cooking, humming the old Irish airs as she worked and never seeking reward. I told her, sure we'd see the film, but it would have to be another day, as I had an appointment that afternoon.

It was not an appointment, exactly, I was going round to the Irish club. Months had gone by since last I was there. When I lost my job, the boys were great to begin with, told me I soon would get something else, more worthy of my attainments, bought me drinks and made a fuss of me altogether. It really warmed the heart, how they stood by me then. But after a while they took to melting away at my approach, or huddling up like a rugby scrum, pretending not to see me. They must have known, I would stand my round if I could, and their boycott hurt me deeply. The next thing was, they were passing remarks about some guy they called The Hoover, how he did this and how he did that, a desperate fellow he sounded. I took it all in, but vaguely, not paying much attention. Then one day Matty Burke was called to the phone and he left down his pint on the bar till he answered. Immediately there was a chorus of 'Mind yourself, Matty, The Hoover will get it', with a great roar of laughter and everyone looking at me.

This was past all enduring. Once, just one single time, distracted by all the worry and grief, I had swallowed a pint that belonged to another man, without the remotest idea of what I was doing; and now this cruel insulting label was pinned to my back for good. I swept out of the place, vowing never to set foot there again.

But there was no sense in hugging old grievances with everything so wonderfully changed. I could return there now, holding my head high. I would shame them all, buying round after round, as if they had never uttered that dastardly gibe, humiliating them by sheer generosity. To repay evil with good is the finest of all revenges.

The word *club* suggests all manner of frills, snacks, billiard parlours, armchairs, newspapers, fruit machines and such. The Erin consisted of one simple room, large as a hall, with only a bar that ran the length of it, a coat-rack, a dozen or so stools, and a telly for race meetings or football matches, and a print of the Easter Rising. Formerly we had a carpet, but there were incidents, and the management replaced it with lino. There was a kind of noble austerity about the Erin, an atmosphere of dedication. It was like one of those avant-garde theatres that despise props and settings. The English go for pubs with pictures on the wall, flowers, brasses, hunting-horns, the devil knows what, distracting to the serious drinker and a real fright when you've taken a few and the room is going round. Here all was plain, bare and dignified, and you could enjoy yourself in comfort.

I had looked for a triumphal coming home but the Club was empty, except for the barman dozing on a barrel behind a squadron of dirty glasses. It was an extraordinary thing, at half-past three on a work-day afternoon. Conor, the barman, seemed annoyed, as if he had expected to finish his nap out in peace, and never gave me the Welcome Back. He had the silvery hair and chubby rosy face that you think would go with benevolence, but he was pure undiluted vinegar all the way through.

'Hallo, stranger,' he said with a yawn, slowly rising from the barrel. 'What'll it be?'

'I'll try a glass of Scotch,' I told him.

'Glass, is it? A large one?'

I considered the query impertinent and unprofessional. It was due to *force majeure* that I was drinking halves, and beer at that, in time gone by and anyway it was none of a barman's business. 'Why wouldn't it be?' I said with hauteur, producing one of the tenners. 'Anything strange about that?'

'Okay, okay.'

'And I'll have a soda through it.'

'Okay.'

'And a packet of Gauloises, and a tin of cheroots.'

'Jesus!' said Conor. 'Fall in for money, did you?'

I ignored this further impudence and drank the Scotch. Conor climbed back on the barrel, dismissing me from his thoughts. As soon as he was comfortably settled and his eyes were shut, I shoved the glass across the bar and snapped, '*When* you're ready.'

He treated me to a baleful glare, but there was nothing he could do.

'You're quiet this evening, all the same,' I said, lighting a Gauloise. As the malt soaked in I began to feel more amiable, prepared to relax and conciliate. 'Where are the boys?'

'Where d'you think?' he returned sourly. 'In the procession.'

Holy Mary! What with the pace of events, I had clean forgotten Corpus Christi. There was to be a mammoth procession of Ireland's faithful from St Peter's in Camden Town to the Holy Thorn in the Archway Road, with two bishops and clergy galore, the confraternity to which I belonged and, it was hoped, thousands of others; and we'd all be on television. The move-off was scheduled for two-thirty sharp, so that most likely it had started, and it would take half an hour to get there: in fact, there was no point in my going now. And I had never so much as got Mass in the morning. On this day of days, when my especial thanks were due to God's Mother for mercy and help, I had failed in even that primary obligation.

'Oh, I'm a nice one!' I groaned. 'I promised them to be there. They were mad for all the men to show up, not leave it to the women as usual. And bless me if I didn't forget!'

'A bloody show-off, if you're asking me,' growled Conor.

'Ah now!'

'Did you ever go on a Corpus Christi at home?'

Well, I didn't. No one had ever exhorted me to, as here. We were to show the godless English that Ireland clung to the Faith and looked towards the Eternal: we were to affirm our role as a spiritual leaven in all this pagan dough. At home there was no such incentive, what with the whole bloody crowd being Catholics too.

'I did, of course, never missed,' I assured him. 'When you're ready.' For I had to get the six o'clock Mass, which meant no more drink after five, and so there wasn't a moment to lose.

'Best thing is, you'd buy the bottle. Then I can take me

139

ease. There'll be a proper dogfight in here, once the procession is over.'

I agreed to that, for Conor was but a poor conversationalist, and he got on the barrel again. I drank away, timing it carefully, finishing the bottle on the stroke of five. It was grand to be drinking Scotch in bulk, after the long bitter period of famine. Apart from the evening at Khan's and the few short ones with Penelope, it had been beer beer beer for months, and beer is what I could never warm to. From the Erin I went on to the Park and strolled up and down to clear my head until it was time for Mass.

At the Oratory I poured out my loving thanks to the Mother of God for her care, entreating her to overlook my forgetfulness earlier on. I also prayed with all my heart for Penelope. And afterwards, as I was leaving, didn't I run into the same dear creature, who had been there all the while! It was a joyful thing to find her a Catholic, another barrier down. She was a bit awkward at first, touchy, because I didn't come back and take the Khans away. Apparently I had said something to make her imagine I would. But I talked her round, gave her some flowers and bought her a drink, and soon we were getting on like a house on fire.

All my hard feelings about her were gone. When I forgive, I do it freely and absolutely. No trace of rancour for the loss of my job or her cold snubbing manner to me was left behind. We are none of us perfect, and it is only Christian to search out the good rather than pounce on the evil. The page was turned, and all my thoughts at present were fixed on the future.

*

The next day began with an awful shock. As usual, unless my health is impaired, I was dressed and shaved by eleven and ready for a pick of breakfast at the Cypriot café. But when I got down to the hall there was a communication for me, John Cruise, directed to Norfolk House itself. I was still using

Norah's address for my scraps of correspondence and any replies that came she forwarded on. Apart from her and the Khans, only Brooke the agent should have known where to find me and I thought at first he was off again, with another string of rules and objections. Then I saw that it came from the Borough Town Hall, and I can tell you, it put the heart across me.

There was nothing to signify in it, only a lot of tomfool questions about my personal affairs, such as people are always asking over here. But how in the name of God did they know of my whereabouts? Or, for the matter of that, of my existence? It is an awful thing for a man to feel he is watched by an army of faceless spies. Suppose they linked up with the Social Security lot! or the lads who kept on sending notices, c/o Norah, to attend at this or that Court on such and such a day. It was just the kind of thing they would do. The papers go on about the Russians, how there comes a knock at the door, and men are dragged from their homes, torn from their loved ones, sent to misery and exile, probably death. Very indignant about it, those hypocrites are; and what is it all the time, but the pot calling the kettle black?

I wanted no breakfast after that. I hurried back up and knocked on Penelope's door, but in vain. At intervals through the day I tried, without success. She was gadding about and amusing herself, when I needed her to tell me how these bloodhounds had picked up my trail. By the time that the evening came, my nerves were shot to pieces. I would have gone round to Norah if her manner had not been so strange when we said goodbye at Santorelli. Perhaps she had wanted me to fix a date for the cinema there and then. I'd have done it too, but there was so much going just now. I was afraid of a disappointment. Out of consideration for her I had left it open, the way she needn't be standing in the foyer and wondering what delayed me.

Well, there I was, fretting, when all of a sudden Penelope appeared at *my* door. I tackled her at once about the questionnaire and she was really obtuse. All she said was that everyone else had got one and thrown it away, and I should do likewise. That the Town Hall was a hotbed of espionage left her unmoved, in fact, she seemed to think it natural. Nothing I had to say made the least impression. Of course I did not mention my reasons for avoiding the limelight, but merely complained on the grounds of principle; and it shocked me to find an Englishwoman so indifferent to that.

She was nice all the same, listening and giving me drinks. I had asked, could we go to her flat, as my own was not yet suitable for receiving guests. There is no doubt of it, drink is a marvellous thing, cushioning us from the blows of life or removing us from their reach altogether. What with the Scotch and the pleasant surroundings and Penelope's own unshakable calm, after a while my fears receded. Remembering my manners, I asked her about herself and where she had been all the day; and without the least little swank or swagger she told me she had spent the afternoon with Caroline Bigge.

'The novelist?' I exclaimed. 'Do you know her?'

'We were at school together,' she replied, as if it were nothing out of the way.

At school with the famous Caroline Bigge! That was the kind of world Penelope came from. And I imagined she was a nobody, but for her winning the Pools. They would have gone to Roedean, or some other classy joint, where everyone was Lady this or the Honourable that . . .

'She is coming here next week,' Penelope went on. 'Would you like to meet her? I called at your flat to ask, but you were so full of your spies and informers.'

Would I like to meet her! All my life I was starving to know celebrities. I felt that my place was among them. As a child I had a favourite daydream, when my two parents fell dead and a nobleman took me into his castle, to bring me up in luxury as a son. There I moved on equal terms with the upper crust and was truly at home, as I never could be in our family house, where not a plate but was chipped, the chairs were mended with string, the doors stood open to all weathers, the hens clucked about on the kitchen floor and my father streeled in, drunk, from the local pub. But real as the castle was to me, with its banquets and butlers, it was all in my head. The world of Caroline Bigge was actual, solid, and Penelope had opened the door to it.

Once, only once, I risked going up in a plane, when I had to or miss an Ireland-England football match, and I never forgot it. By way of precaution I had confessed and received, and in the aircraft I held on to the rosary in my trouser pocket, but I was desperately scared all the same. There was the usual summer sky over Dublin airport, grey, shaggy, weeping, and the idea of being swallowed up in all that murk was dreadful. As we bounded upward, the clouds swirled about the windows, black as night; but then, in a moment or two, there were flickers of sun and the clouds thinned out. A few moments more and we were above them altogether, with the sun pouring down and the sky a radiant blue.

The wonder of that swift easy transformation, I was experiencing again now. Just as in the plane, so with a few casual words from Penelope, I shot from a familiar greyness to a magic world of space and light. Things I had longed for and that seemed out of reach, suddenly were to be mine. I stood on the threshold of a new existence. Caroline would take to me, of that I felt sure; she would admit me to her friendship and to the brilliant circles in which she moved. I chattered away like an excited boy, while Penelope looked motherly and amused. I tore up the questionnaire, amazed that I had ever allowed such a trifle to worry me. Then I took myself off, to feast on my prospects alone. There were six whole days to go before the meeting took place, and I hardly knew how I should ever get through them.

Four

It was a curious thing that, observant as I am, I had never before noticed the expression of the eyes now looking out into mine. Their colour and form and their fringe of long dark lashes were a source of pleasure whenever I saw them, but that was purely external. This morning, however, as I shaved, I happened to look upward and meet their level gaze in the mirror. They were full of a brooding tenderness, like that of a mother who contemplates her child. I stood there, communing with them, thinking how little we know of ourselves; and my thoughts went continually back to them as I finished dressing and prepared for the day.

I took my usual egg and chips at the Cypriot café and went on down to the King's Road. It had occurred to me during the night that I must smarten myself up before Caroline saw me. Elegance was frowned on at the Bank, for fear of the customers taking fright, and clerks were required to dress 'discreetly' in suits of grey or blue. Mr Goodge, I am sure, would have preferred us all in the alpaca jackets and sponge-bag trousers he wore himself, like the museum-piece that he was. When he interviewed me for the job, he said I would have to do something about my clothes, as 'this isn't a racecourse, you know.' So much for my Donegal tweeds, that the boys in Dublin were mad for! But it wasn't the moment to answer back, and I got something off the peg that would have cast a gloom at a funeral. After I left the Bank, of course, there was no cash to remedy matters. Finbar begged my tweeds from me, and I was stuck with the penitential grey ever since. But, thanks to God and His blessed Mother, money was plentiful now and I intended to burst forth like a butterfly from the cocoon.

As I wandered past the shops, however, looking at the gay assortment of shirts, kaftans, cowboy outfits, spangled denims and high-heeled boots. I found myself in a quandary. I wanted to do Penelope proud, all right, but it was Caroline that I hoped to impress. Intuition told me that it was she, not Penelope, who had proposed our meeting. Penelope would have been talking about me, praising my looks or passing on some witty remark that I had made, and Caroline would have said, 'I should like to know that man!' The more I thought of it, the more certain I felt that this was true. Even if they were at school together, Penelope must be in awe of so famous a woman and would hardly go introducing people right and left unless she were asked. No: something Caroline had heard had gone down well: I had, unbeknown to myself, made a hit with her; and it was for me to follow through and consolidate the position.

But I hadn't an idea in the world what to get. It was chancy, dressing for someone I did not know, whose tastes I must somehow or other divine. From her photograph, she herself had a predilection for fancy things, Hungarian blouses, African robes, but who was to say if she would like them on me? And I felt in my bones that this first encounter was crucial. I could picture the scene exactly, myself coming in, Penelope introducing us, Caroline running a sharp eye over me, deciding at once if I came up to scratch. A wrong move here, an error of judgement, and all that Penelope had said in my favour might go for nothing. It was sad to think of so much depending on trifles, but that is the way of the world.

Well, I was puzzling over the matter and just about losing heart when I got an inspiration. Among the reviews of Caroline's new book I had seen one, by an Anthony Something, that was snide and disparaging. A remark of his came suddenly to mind now: 'The hero has no appeal whatever for me but it is clear, from her fond and detailed descriptions, that Miss Bigge is greatly enamoured of him.' So all I had to do was run to the Public Library and ask for the novel. The fond descriptions in question would soon put me right.

At the Library there was the inevitable English fuss and obstruction. I had no card, I was not a householder, Arabella Road was not in the area, fiction was not given out in the Reference Reading Room, this particular title was in any case new, with a long waiting list . . . Really, they'd make you sick. I was arguing away and beginning to shout when a new voice beside me took up the cudgels on my behalf.

'It's because he's Irish, isn't that right?' it demanded in a good Cork accent. 'We'll go to the Race Relations Board!'

And, bless me, if it wasn't my old boyhood friend Benedict Geraghty! the one I mentioned earlier, as being in the counterfeit banknotes line. He was looking much as usual, pale and studious like something out of a seminary, only with a bit of a hunted air, and clutching a fat parcel done up in brown paper. He always did the talking at the Christian Brothers and I was well content to leave it to him now.

'Nothing of the kind,' the librarian said, but you could see she was rattled. 'The rules are the same for all.'

'In me eye!' quoth Benedict. 'Don't cod me. We've only to open our gobs and down come the shutters. Now give us that book, or we'll go to the Board. The days when you rode roughshod over the likes of us are past.'

He spoke grimly, throwing himself into the act, and the librarian got all pink and tremulous.

'I'm not riding over anyone, just telling you what the rules are,' she pleaded. 'And we are the Reference Room. There are no novels in here.'

'Then how do you know there's people waiting for this one?' Bendy snapped. He should have been a lawyer. 'You have it all right, but you won't let it go. Come on, Johnny, we'll see what the Board has to say.' And turning on his heel he marched for the door, with me behind him trying not to laugh.

'Hold on a minute, please, don't go yet,' the librarian quavered after us. She was a thin spent little woman of fifty or so, that couldn't say boo to a goose. 'If you would kindly wait here, I'll speak to the superintendent.'

So we graciously consented to give her another chance. Away she went, and in a few minutes came back with the book in her hands, the carry-on having all been for show. We had won, without firing a shot! It would stagger you, thinking how paper tigers like these once ruled the world.

'The Superintendent says you may have this, as an exception,' she said, all effusive and anxious to please. 'Would you be good enough to sign for it? Thank you *so* much!'

It was quite a time since the two of us had met, and there was a lot to talk over. Bendy asked what in the name of God I wanted with the book and I said I had taken up literature. Then I asked what *he* was doing in the library, and he said he was checking a Latin quotation. Fair enough, as I say, there's no point in coming out with all you have on your mind.

We went down the King's Road, taking it easy, a pint here and a pint there, until, in the Lord Nelson, the first closing bell rang. We tried to get a last drink, like everyone else, but the barman said we'd had enough and told us to scarper. Bendy tried the Race Relations Board, but he was Irish himself bad luck to him. He only said what to do with it and to leave at once if we didn't want him to help us.

We could have gone to the Erin, but the notion took me to show Bendy my flat. Last time he saw me I was out of a job and broke, and he despised me for a mug when I wouldn't join in his financial dealings. I wanted him to know that a man could go straight and still come up in the world. So we took a taxi to Norfolk House and, I must say, it bowled him over. I had never been able to impress him before, even at school he was blasé and knew it all better, but he went from room to room and looked at the views from the windows and agreed it was gorgeous.

It was too late for lunch. I opened a bottle of malt and we drank away with a will. It made a powerful mixture with all the Guinness we had inside us, and we soon began to warm up.

I rattled on about my dreams for the future, and he played back with the Christian Brothers and the grand old days in Cork. From there, we went on to religion, and my memory of our remarks is somewhat blurred. I can just recall Bendy commiserating with God, poor devil, over the sins of the world before he made a dash for the toilet; but after that all is a blank. When or how he left, I cannot say. I woke up to find the place in darkness and myself lying stretched on the floor.

The drink was dying by now, but I felt pretty cheap and I crawled straight to my bed and took what ease I could. It wasn't the best night's sleep but I'd never have closed an eye at all if I'd known what was to confront me in the morning. That bloody old eedjit Bendy had gone off with my book and left his own parcel behind him! Well, that was not too bad itself, but when I opened the parcel to see was there anything in the way of an address, it was nothing but ten pound notes! He'd been dragging this little fortune all over London—I'd noticed how he clung to it, never leaving it out of his hand for a moment wherever we stopped—and then, just for the few drinks in him, he'd left it with me in exchange for a novel by Caroline Bigge! It was the kind of thing that could turn a man teetotal.

I hadn't an idea where Bendy was living now, and it was looking for trouble to leave the package in at the Irish Club. He'd be on to me fast enough once he sobered up and realised what he'd done, so I just tied the parcel again and hid it, waiting for his frantic tattoo on the door. But nothing happened all day and towards evening, my head having cleared a little, I set off for the Cypriots and a fry-up. It is a curious medical fact that soggy chips and greasy rashers have a pacific effect on a tormented inside.

On the way I bought an evening paper and bless me if it wasn't featuring Bendy, slap on the front page. On leaving me, it appeared, he'd tangled with a cop and been taken in; and, once at the station, they had somehow connected him with other graver matters—they didn't say which—and there he now sat, 'helping the police with their inquiries'. A nice dope I felt. It shows the evil effects of drink, that up to this minute it never so much as crossed my mind that the notes in the parcel were forged and that Bendy must have been on a job.

My first reaction was one of panic. I didn't like all that about helping with the inquiries. Supposing the fuzz roughed Bendy up and to buy them off he said something to implicate me? But then, what could he say? I had gone to the library to change a book and there run across my old boyhood friend, reading Catullus. We'd had a few drinks together, and then he'd gone home, forgetting a parcel which I put aside unexamined. That was my account of things and no one was going to shake it.

But as I sat in the café, waiting for the fry and listening to the fruit machines, I began to worry again. It is the drawback of an imagination like mine. You get marvellous insights and visions, true, but you are also a prey to doubts and fears that duller people are spared. If Bendy dragged me in and the police came nosing round, might they not link me with the Social Security hullabaloo? My name was probably on one of their rotten lists by now. And if, on the top of that, they found the notes on the premises, and then stumbled across my own little nest-egg, wouldn't they leap to conclusions? Pull me in to the cells, burn me with cigarettes, leap up and down on my stomach, even fasten on me some crime they hadn't been able to solve?

The best plan was to destroy the notes altogether and know nothing about them if asked. As soon as I got to the flat I took out the parcel with this in view, only to realise that it was easier said than done. There was no open fireplace where I could burn it. Then I had a brainwave. I put it in one of the plastic bags they use for garbage and took it down to the area for collection. But the area shed, where the dustbins are, was locked, and there was a notice on the door to say the dustmen were striking again. Honest to God, they're more often out than in. Tenants were requested to bring their garbage to one of the emergency dumps outside, to be taken away by contract. The inconvenience was regretted.

You could say that again. It was like trying to dispose of a body. Off I went to the specified dump, only to find a couple of fellows rummaging in the contents as if they expected to quarry a diamond tiara. I hurried on to the next one in Agincourt Square, and here was a cop leaning right up against it with an air of having settled in for the night.

By now I was too weary to traipse around any more and I decided to call it a day. There was no real hurry after all. The cops would need a search warrant before they did themselves any good, and tomorrow was Sunday. Time enough to sleep on it.

Back in the flat I left the plastic bag lolling in a corner of the kitchen like any old trash and poured myself a nightcap. One thing led to another and soon I felt on top of the world again, a match for the best and afraid of nothing. My thoughts turned to the notes themselves, which so far I hadn't really studied. To take one out and compare it with the genuine article would be a kind of game to play with myself, like those puzzles they have in magazines. What is Wrong with this Picture?

You wouldn't believe it, but I couldn't detect a single flaw anywhere. Colour, printing, watermarks, all seemed genuine, and don't forget, I was a specialist, this was my job. Even the paper was right. I took a note in my two hands and tugged on it several times, as if to tear it asunder, and the feel, the resistance, the sound like a flapping sail, all was just as it should be. Then I got out a fistful and told them over, in rapid cashier-style, and again I would have sworn that they were real.

I now began to muse in philosophical vein on the nature of truth and falsehood. If indeed these spurious notes were in every respect the counterpart of the others, what was the difference between them? I could see none. And in that case, where was the harm in passing them on? You did no wrong to the fellow that took them, for he could pass them on as well, getting value the same as yourself, and with no more fear of detection. To all intents and purposes, they were sound Treasury issue—and, but for the grace of God, I should have thrown them away!

As always, when fortune smiles on me, I felt humble and devout rather than brashly cockahoop. It filled me with awe to think how, once again, I had been watched over and protected. Those lads, that cop, who had scared me away from the dumps, had been sent for a purpose. Now I turned the whole lot of Bendy's notes on to the table and counted them. There were a hundred and twenty in it, half as much again as Penelope had paid on behalf of the Khans. Reverently I gathered the money up and placed it with my own in the Bank's leather bag. If Bendy shakes off the police and comes looking for it, I will tell him I got rid of it; and if he cuts up rough, I will say how passing counterfeit notes is a serious business and I acted in his own best interests, like the friend I always was.

Five

Up to this point my story has largely been of sordid things, disasters, humiliations, encounters with low-class people and the desperate makeshifts to which a man may be driven by undeserved misfortune. Now I felt that I could turn my back on all that. Aside from this new miraculous windfall, there was the meeting with Caroline Bigge only a few days off and this was to bring me into another world altogether. I resolved to put those days to good use preparing myself, shunning my usual haunts with their dangerous companions, avoiding the Irish Club like the plague, holding aloof even from Norah, and thinking how to appear to the best advantage before the famous Carol.

I was busy on this at Mass, one of the Low ones that let me in for a sermon. There was some old boy from an African mission, droning on and appealing for funds, but his problems didn't concern me. Of course I remembered to thank the Blessed Virgin for the signal favour she had once more conferred, but on the whole my thoughts were secular. And I skipped the Corpus Christi procession that followed too. My heart wasn't in it today and anyhow, it was a piddling affair compared to the first and no one from TV was bothering.

Near the church was a newspaper stand, where as a rule on Sunday morning I bought the *Catholic Herald* and the *News of the World*. This time I took the *Observer* and *The Sunday Times*, classy yokes both of them, hoping to find some more about Carol in them and also to fill myself in on the cultural scene. Her book was advertised all right, with inches and inches of what the critics had said, but there was nothing else about her. In fact, the book pages were a drag from my point of view. There were lists of novels reviewed by guys who seemed to think they could have done them all better, and otherwise it was mostly political or airy-fairy.

It was reading the arty page of one or the other that I got a great idea of how to present myself to Carol. Here was an article about an exhibition of paintings by some wop, still life they called it, lemons, garlic, grapes, stuff like that. It appeared, the fellow had done such a fancy job on the garlic and grapes as to put over, the critic said, the 'kind of radiance which seems to come from within, a glow that has nothing to do with surface colour. Yet surface colour is all the artist has to work with, and Signore Pirrone's triumphant use of it to achieve his desired effect points to a rare artistic sensibility and a perfect mastery of technique.'

Wow! that was something for me. From the start I had realised the importance of figuring as a Some-one, qualified to meet Caroline on her own level, not as just another gushing admiring fan. I had to step into the picture as of right. Then why not introduce myself as a fellow artist, though working in a different field? I have already mentioned the notable powers that I possessed, had I only cared to exercise them: so that no actual deceit was involved.

Not only would she be immediately drawn to me by sympathy, but it would solve the problem of what I should wear. I would go tomorrow to that shop in Chelsea with paints, easels, brushes and smocks in the window and fix myself up. I simply couldn't imagine how this plan could fail. If she wanted to see my work, I could tell her there was nothing finished on hand, as a whole collection had recently gone off to one of the galleries.

It would do me a power of good with Penelope too, I reckoned, because girls like her are always mad for art and artists. Of course there was a touch of risk where she was concerned, for she had been to the flat and there was no studio, and also, she could be wondering why this was the first she had heard of my painting at all. And there was the future to think of, on the top of that. Once we were engaged, I would somehow have to explain it all away, unless I wanted the sweat of turning to and actually knocking the masterpieces out.

But I told myself to cool it and not to let my imagination take over. I had never been in such a fix that I couldn't talk my way out. All that mattered at present was the approach to Carol, and I was certain of having picked a winner there. And all that was needed was the confidence to make it work. Confidence is the greatest gift a man can have. Life is a species of tight-rope act, lose your nerve, hesitate, wobble and off you come. You have to look ahead of you calmly, step out as if you were on the earth below, not balancing on a rope, and never think of the height or how far there would be to fall.

I read the article again and again until I nearly had it by heart and could patter smoothly on in a similar key. In the morning I went to buy the smock and some paints to smear down the front, also a floppy bow tie and a pair of sandals, such as artists wear. I wanted to look the part to perfection. It was too bad my hair wasn't longer and that there wasn't time to grow a beard, but you can't have it all. My brain was constantly humming with new ideas for making the affair a success. I would take Carol a bunch of flowers, to flatter her and show my interest; but I would also—and this was a subtle move—arrive very late, giving as the excuse that my work had so absorbed me, everything else went out of my head. She would, I felt sure, respect me for that. She would see that I had bigger things on my mind than a social occasion, even with somebody famous in it.

Well, the evening came and I heard the lift bring Caroline up. She was to get her dinner there and I was to go in for drinks at half-nine. When it was that, it needed all my self-control to stick to the plan and not go rushing in at once. And I was feeling terribly nervous, not a bit like myself, I suppose because it was all so important to me, so much depended on it. I didn't dare take a drink either, in case I couldn't help but take some others, and then maybe lose the thread of what I wanted to say.

At half-ten I could bear it no longer and, seizing the bunch of flowers, presented myself at the flat next door. My heart was beating wildly and I scarcely knew what I did. When Penelope opened, I just tore past her and into the room where Caroline Bigge was sitting.

What followed then was one of the cruellest things that ever befell me. I'll have to knock off for a while and compose myself, till I get the strength to continue.

*

A bird soars and wheels in the air, wings stretched wide, plumage iridescent in the rays of the sun. A shot, and it plunges to earth, lifeless, a tangle of bloodied feathers. That is the image that springs up whenever I recall the ruin of my hopes and dreams that night.

It is easy now, afterwards, to realise where my plan went wrong. I had made it in ignorance of the true nature of Caroline Bigge. I had expected her to be warm, sensitive, human, alive to quality in others and free from any taint of meanness, a kindred soul in fact. But she was cold, conceited and destructive. She stared at me ironically, as if I were a joke, and also suspiciously, as if I might be up to no good.

I got an inkling of what she was the moment I gave her the flowers. She thanked me in a perfunctory way, with a sort of grin on her chops, as if she despised them and as if people mostly gave her orchids or roses at a couple of pounds a stem. These were simple yokes off a barrow, but lovely all the same, like everything else God ever created. Why spend a fortune at some classy joint in the Brompton Road when something as good is going for 50p? To me the meanest flower that blows can give thoughts that do often lie too deep for tears. I'm not sure if that is my own, or did I read it somewhere, but it's the philosophy I go on when buying a bunch for a lady.

As I say, that gave me a hint of her personality, but it was nothing to what came after. Now I gave her the spiel about my painting, how it wouldn't come right, how Art was a hard mistress but I could serve no other. I had rehearsed it so often the words tripped out of themselves, but I suffered badly from stage fright just the same and it was a relief to get it done.

I don't remember exactly what she said, but it sounded sympathetic: how it didn't matter, the picture came first, and I had chosen a wonderful subject. I thought that here was where we kicked off to the serious conversation I'd been hankering for, and I was carrying it on from there, about loving a challenge and easy things being not worth while, when her eyes met mine and I saw from the cruel mockery in them that she didn't believe a single word I had said!

Reader, there was no mistaking it. I had seen that look in English eyes before. It was like the newspaper all over again, the one I offered the IRA feature to. Blatant disbelief, without any attempt to conceal it. And words can hardly describe what it does to a proud and sensitive Irishman. It is as if he had a heel rubbed raw and somebody kicked him on it.

Gravely wounded though I was, my self-respect would not allow me to take this lying down. If I were to swallow an affront so enormous, I could never hold my head up again. That the story of my painting happened to be an invention was neither here nor there. She could not possibly have known that it was. If it had been truth itself, and me with twenty pictures on view at the Tate, she would still have given me that nasty sneering look, because that is the kind of bitch she is.

To tax her with it, have it out, argue with or upbraid her, was beneath me. Instead, I would cut her down to size. The best way to shrink this egomaniac, used to flattery and the limelight wherever she went, was not to have heard of her before. Or so I reasoned.

'Penny tells me you write,' I began, after thinking fast for a moment or two. 'I'm afraid I don't know your name. Should I?'

That 'Should I?', in my opinion, was a stroke of genius. First, I said it in the tone of voice that implies a knowledge of any names at all worth knowing. And then, it was an awkward kind of question to answer. 'Of course you should!'—the woman would hardly have the gall to say that. Most likely she would colour up and make some feeble reply, with the wind taken out of her sails and her confidence ebbing to zero.

But I had miscalculated again, again through my ignorance of the creature. Far from my query putting her out, she seemed to be expecting it and to find it amazingly funny.

'No indeed,' she said, with a supercilious smile. 'I didn't know yours till just now.'

That sneer was too much for me altogether. She was throwing the mask aside now, coming into the open, deriding me for my obscurity, my lack of achievement, as if not to be written about in the papers meant that you were a nobody. My outstanding potential, that of all people a novelist should have realised at once, had escaped her completely.

By now I was fairly boiling inside, and my recollection of what followed may be a little blurred. I believe I told her that I didn't read novels, as being only suited to women . . . yes, that's it, and she said, 'But can you read at all?' So then I really let fly, I let her have it. I told her I was a great reader when books were worth reading, and also what my teachers at school had thought of my literary gifts, only the great things to say had all been said and I had better sense than to chew them over again. Then she laughed right into my face and came back with another gibe or two.

If a man had spoken as she did, I would have knocked the living daylights out of him. As it was, with a supreme effort, I pulled myself together. I wiped the floor with her, but as a gentleman does, without raising my voice or displaying emotion. 'Madam,' I said calmly, getting up from my chair, 'I can see that you are not yourself. To continue our conversation would be disagreeable to you and inconsiderate of me.' With that, I bowed to both the ladies and quietly left the room.

I felt sure Penelope would follow me and try to make it up. That her friend's outrageous conduct surprised and distressed her had been written all over her face. No doubt, until this evening, she had been as unaware of the woman's nature as I myself. The revelation must have come as a brutal shock, and it was only fair that I should be understanding with her, and generous. Before I ever reached my flat, I was thinking what to say, looking for words to comfort her and free her from any sense of guilt.

The thought of my own benevolence and of the superb exit I had made restored my good humour. But Penelope did not come and did not come, and at last I grew angry again. It must be, this famous woman was so important to her that she would let anything pass before she'd risk a falling-out. That is the way of the world.

Just the same, I would give her a last chance. I wrote her a moderate and reasonable little note, explaining that the treatment received in her house was such as a man of honour could hardly overlook and asking for an apology if she desired our friendship to continue. I could do no more : few would have done as much.

Believe it or not, there was no reply. I slipped the note under her door when she went down with Caroline to see her off, and stood waiting inside my own, hardly breathing, expecting her to knock. Nothing happened. After an age, as it seemed, I went to the windows and looked out. No light came from hers. She had gone to bed. Now I realised that she and the Bigge were birds of a feather. All my dreams lay in ruins about me. All my innocent aspirations had come to nothing. My mind was in agony. Something of what passed in it, you will have found in the Foreword to this memoir.

But the last word in all this shall be mine, of that I am resolved.

Six

One of the torments of my life when things are going badly is to dream that all is well. I have already described how I would dream of finding or winning money all that time I was headed for the rocks. It has always been thus, ever since I was a boy. At school, when we were in for a hiding, we got it on Friday afternoon before our confession, which gave us anything up to four and a half days to savour the treat in advance. Every night I would dream that it was called off, or that the strap was missing, or that, when I went to the study, Brother Gabriel gave me something to eat instead. Once I dreamed that he had turned into a Presentation nun. I would wake and lie there smiling, until suddenly the awful truth sank in. Brother Gabriel played hockey for Ireland and his punishments were a fright; but the waiting for them was worst of all. And yet I have no hard feelings against him now. I tell myself that, without him, I might never have become the man I am.

And so it happened the night after the party. Again and again, when at last I got to bed, I dreamed that all had gone according to plan, with Carol bowled over and Penelope dumbly admiring us both. In one of those dreams Carol gave me a book of hers, bound in leather, and when I opened it there was an inscription, *To the new Michael Angelo*, in letters of red and gold. Then I had to awake to the memory of her stinging contempt, her dismissal of me as good for nothing except to laugh at, to act as a butt for her cruel sneers. I tossed and turned, smarting under it, until I dropped off once more to find her wreathed in smiles anew, all honey and invitations.

Round about ten I got up, with no particular ideas of how

I should spend the day. The smock was lying on the floor beside the bed and I gave it a savage kick. That caused a shooting pain in my temples, and I went to the kitchen to look for a cure. Thanks be to God, there were a few bottles left of the strong dark ale I got in after the session with Bendy, it's something no one should ever be without.

Far from clearing my brain, however, it must have stopped it from working normally. Penelope had partly shown herself in her true colours when she failed to respond to my offer of reconciliation the night before. But during one of my wakeful periods I had realised that she was even worse than I supposed. She had not allowed Caroline to insult me because she was too much awed by her to protest. No! she knew her friend well and had brought her there for that very purpose. Why she did this to a man who wished only her good, who had believed himself in love with her and was ready to make her his wife, is one of those terrible things in human nature that nobody can explain. Not I, at least, the simple and trusting fellow. Perhaps a headshrinker could.

As I say, this had been perfectly clear to me before. But now my poor intellect, enfeebled by the beer, set off in a zany dance of its own. It told me, all was not lost, that Penelope, having slept upon it, would have come to a better frame of mind. It reminded me of how eager she had been to help the Khans in their distress. It maintained that a woman who forked out eight hundred pounds at the drop of a hat could not be wicked right through. It urged me to shave, dress, go out for a bunch of the flowers she loved so well and try my luck again.

I say 'my poor intellect', but perhaps it was the *alter ego* that we all carry round inside us, the one that is always butting in and answering back, or telling us to do the opposite of what we know is wise. Anyhow, I took its advice as usual. When I got to the flower barrow, the lad was stuffing a last bunch of the flowers I wanted into a litterbin near by and he had nothing left but roses and sweet peas without any prices on them, a sure indication of expense.

'Hold on there,' I said. 'Let me have those.'

'You agine,' he commented. 'But these are past it, guvnor. They're the sime as wot you ad yesterday.'

'They're what my girl friend fancies.'

'Gaillardias are? Go on!' he said, in his cheeky London way. 'Wish my old woman was alf as easy.' But he took them out and wrapped them for me. 'Ow about some nice sweet peas to go with um? Last a fortnight, they will.'

'Sweet peas give her a headache,' I informed him. 'What's this I owe you?'

'Oh, I coulden charge for the likes of them. Tell you wot, guvnor, ask me to the weddin.'

That was fine. But when the door of Penelope's flat was opened to me, there was a disagreeable surprise. Instead of herself, a frog-faced old woman with her hair done up in curlers appeared and told me Miss B. was out. No, she hadn't said when she'd be back, just went off abrupt, not like her, as a rule she stayed for a chat, she must have urgent business, was there a message? I replied that I was the man from next door, and had brought these flowers after a little tiff we'd had, or some such yarn. Either I said more than I intended or she read a whole lot into it, for she gave me a vulgar wink and suggested I come in and wait.

I decided it would be as well, having screwed myself up to the point of coming at all. If I went back now, I'd only continue the cure and end up fit for nothing. The hag took me into the kitchen and sat me down while she went on with the dishes left from the evening before. The way those London women do, she drowned me in a torrent of talk, to which however after a minute or two I ceased to listen, being busy with thoughts of my own.

Seeing those beautiful plates and the cut glass and the silver revived all the tenderness I had felt for Penny, and the longing to make her mine. And that part of my brain, or the *alter ego*, or whatever it was that had brought me here, whispered that it still might be. My critical faculties were fast asleep. I began dreaming of our life together, of how we should spend our time, of the little arrangements we should make. Penny would allow me so much a year, a couple of thousand or so paid into my own personal account. A man needs independence, if he is to be respected as the head of a family. He cannot go running to his wife for a few pounds here and a few pounds there, have her settling small bills and maybe asking questions about them. Such things would strike at the very root of our love, for a woman is never happy unless she looks up to her man.

It might be for the best, my *alter ego* mused, if I took charge of her money altogether. With my financial acumen and the knowledge of her affairs that I gained through working at the Bank, I could relieve her of that burden. It would be my contribution, placing me on an equal footing, and as no mere cake-eating gigolo. She would have her riding, her books, her music, the household to run, things more suited to a lovely girl than puzzling her head over taxes and dividends . . .

Here a telephone squawked in another room, bringing me down to earth.

'That's the telephone,' the cleaner revealed. 'Never stops this morning, my word.' She bustled off and presently came back. 'Telegram from our Aunt Rosemary, coming to stay. More bleeding work. And before that, new clothes ready, and an appointment for a hair-do . . . Our young Lady's sweet on some one, I shouldn't wonder.' She gave me a leer. 'And a Miss Big, wanting to know how she is. A sekkertary, is what she ought to get.'

She chattered on and on. I stayed a while longer, smoking and dreaming. At last I felt I should really take my hook, since there was no knowing where Penelope was or when she would return. Having impressed on the hag that she must remember to give her my flowers—for which there was no need, as the creature was all agog—I went back home and started dreaming there. But the day passed and there was no sign. Nothing, nothing, nothing, only silence.

Once again, my *alter ego* had played me false.

*

Who was it said, As flies to wanton boys, are we to the gods?
It sounds like Oscar Wilde or Swift, anyway some fellow that
knew his onions. Now I ran into one more patch of trouble,
and all because I wanted to do a kindly deed. In this vale of
tears it is the good we do, not the bad, that we come to repent
of most.

My experience with those two jades turned my thoughts
back to Norah Kilbane, the ever staunch and serviceable. I
remembered all her acts of friendship, great and small, and it
shamed me to think how little I had done to repay her. Apart
from my company, she had nothing from me but that single
lunch at Santorelli. I never took her to the film she wanted to
see, although I considered doing so more than once. They
changed the programme while I was thinking it over.

Now I decided to take her to lunch again, to a real blow-out
this time, none of your plates of spaghetti. At first I thought
we'd go to the Ritz, where I had never been myself, and really
do things in style. It was fun to plan it, how I'd book a table
there without telling her what was up, just putting her in the
taxi and calmly giving the order, 'To the Ritz!' as if I were
in and out of the place all the time. She had never put her
foot through the door there either, of course, and I could just
imagine her, all a-flutter with joy and excitement.

But I pictured the scene so often and so vividly that, by the
time I got round to asking her, I was tired of the whole idea.
Or rather, I felt as if we had actually gone and there was little
point in going again. And then, she'd be out of her depth, she
hadn't the class to carry it off, the waiters would stare and I'd
have to blush for her clothes and her manners and the way she
held her knife and fork, grasping them in her fists like a baby.
A man likes a woman to be a credit to him. So it was back to
Santorelli, and very delighted she was, especially when I told
her to ask for whatever she wanted.

163

'In the money, are you?' she demanded, beaming. 'Is it the horses again, or what?'

That jarred on me a little. One of the admirable things about Norah was, that she never asked any questions. Most women want to know the whys and wherefores of every blessed thing, so you are kept inventing all the time just when you'd rather relax.

'The horses are not unkind,' I answered. 'Now, what'll it be?'

'You say,' she replied. 'I'm sure you know best.'

As a matter of fact, I didn't. The menu was all in Italian, which might as well have been Chinese. But I was glad to see Norah herself again, so I went to work, scanning the list attentively as if it conveyed a whole lot to me.

'Special Today, zuppa inglese,' I read out. 'That means, English soup. Suppose we begin with that?'

'Fine!'

But nothing else was as simple as that. The other time we were here, she took her plate of spaghetti and I had steak and chips. I began to wish we'd gone to the Ritz after all. A waiter came up and stood there with his pencil ready and his head on one side. It was the fellow we got before, and I could see he thought very poorly of us.

'Have you any roast chicken?' I asked him coldly. 'I don't see it here.'

He pointed to an entry on the menu without a word.

'Ah yes,' I hurried on. 'We'll both take that, with all the trimmings. And as a first course, we'll try the zuppa inglese.'

The fool seemed not to understand my pronunciation. I pointed to the menu now, and he smiled as if he were sorry for me.

'Zuppa inglese?' he said, making it sound quite different, not at all the way it was written. 'Is pudding-a. Cake-a, jam-a, rum-a, cream-a.'

'T'isn't!' I said, flaring up, feeling my face burn. 'It's a watercress soup with fried bread snippets.' For I could not allow him to best me in front of Norah.

164

'Is pudding-a,' he repeated. 'I bring *IM after* chicken'. But we have nice-a green-a soup-a too.' He scribbled all this down and started to run away.

'And give us a couple of glasses of sherry, schooners, now!' I bawled after him. 'And a bottle of champagne with the meal!'

Madness. Nothing had been less in my mind than to order a bottle of anything, but I had to show that flunkey the sort of man I was and make him respect me. Norah was staring in a bemused kind of way through her spiky lashes, all glued together with that stuff she will put on. She was impressed, but the waiter merely trotted off as if he hadn't heard.

After a while another fellow came up, in a crimson jacket and with a fancy chain round his neck, and asked if I were the gentleman who wanted champagne. 'We have Pol Roger and Veuve Clicquot,' he said. 'But would you like something cheaper, a non-vintage?'

This new impertinence flicked me on the raw. There seemed to be only rudeness and ignorance wherever I went these days. 'I don't know why you imagine that,' I replied in a cutting voice, looking him up and down.

'Then which of the brands will you have?'

I had already forgotten the names, having never heard of either, but I would have sooner died than ask.

'You can bring a bottle each of the two,' I said, leaning back in my chair and folding my arms, while Norah gave a gasp. She never knows how to conduct herself in the public eye.

'And two schooners of sherry? Dry? medium? sweet?'

God almighty, this was a bloody quiz. I'm not a sherry drinker at all and it was news to me, there being different kinds. 'Whichever one is the best,' I snapped. 'Only bring it at once.'

Apparently he was too grand to do any such thing, for a third menial brought the sherry, and terrible mawkish stuff it was. Then your man wheeled up a trolley with a couple of buckets of water on it, as if we were horses. I thought he was taking the mickey, and was halfway up from my chair to hit him when two lads followed, each with a champagne bottle, and it transpired that the buckets were meant for those. Things like that can only be learned by experience.

In spite of the unfortunate start, I must say it was a really enjoyable meal. Now and again I had to tell Norah to keep her voice down, for she'd go into peals of laughter that made all the people turn round. But the food was prime and the champagne flowed and presently I was on top of the world, with my sorrows pushed to the back of my head and the future smiling again. I got a bit of a knock all the same when they brought the bill, which was for twenty-three pounds. Twenty-three pounds, if you please, for a pick to eat and a sup of wine for two, and with millions starving! But I told myself, we cannot always be pinching and scraping and counting the cost if we are to live our lives to the full, and we are none the worse for breaking out an odd time.

Far from being a case of all well that ends well, however, this was only the hush before the storm. Storm? Hurricane. I paid the bill and got the change and was about to leave when Norah said she must go to the ladies. That meant, as well I knew, she'd prink and powder and paint a full twenty minutes and, at the heel of the hunt, come out with the same old puss she had gone in with. The vanity of homely girls has a peculiar sadness about it.

I sat there chafing, wondering could I decently go without her and deciding I hardly could; which bears out what I was saying just now, about our good deeds making far more mischief than the others. The waiter came sidling back and asked me to step into the office, as Mr Santorelli wished to have a word. I assumed that, after me spending all that money, he was going to say he hoped the meal had been to my liking, or maybe get me to sign the distinguished customer's book, and I gladly agreed. But I saw my mistake the moment I got in the door. The fat little man was at his desk with my three tenners in front of him, and he looked at me with loathing, as if they'd caught me trying to sneak away with the silver.

166

'These notes of yours,' he growled. 'I regret to say, they are bad.'

That was the last thing on earth I expected to hear. By this time I had used quite a few of Bendy's notes and there had been no objection before. 'How do you mean, bad?' I demanded haughtily, while I did some furious thinking.

'I mean bad!' he barked. 'False. Counterfeit. Not genuine.'

'Can't be,' I told him calmly. 'I know for a fact they are good.'

'How do you know? Where did you get them?'

'From a Turf Accountant,' I said, although it was not his place to inquire.

'Aha! So! From a bookie.' He nodded slowly and weightily, as if to say, that settles it.

'Yes, but I checked them over before I left his office,' I went on. 'I know genuine notes from forgeries. I should, by now. I work in a Bank myself.'

'In which Bank?'

'That's my business, if you'll pardon me,' I retorted, amazed at his effrontery and grieved by his mistrust.

'And this is *my* business,' he snarled, tapping the notes. 'I am most sorry for the Bank where you work. Look again,' and he passed one of them over to me. Then he took a tenner out of a drawer and passed that as well. 'Now, a real one. Compare, if you please, the watermarks, the Queen's head, the figure 10. Genuine? Bah!'

Well, I was never so crestfallen or so humiliated in all my life! These were the notes that, after a careful expert scrutiny, I had passed as perfect! and here was a wop restaurant keeper, putting me straight! For what he said was true. Once I compared them, the faults in Bendy's stuck out a mile. It must be, when I examined them first, the booze had affected my judgement.

My poise, my sang-froid, deserted me for once: I could only hang my head and mumble, 'Looks like you're right.'

'It is well!' Santorelli said; but at least the snarl had gone. 'And now?'

I had taken those three notes to cover the lunch and for the afternoon that I was proposing to spend at the Irish Club; but thanks to the Blessed Virgin, who ever has me in her motherly keeping, I also had about me a few of those I got from Penny. It was a terrible wrench, parting with them, but needs must when the devil drives.

'I owe you an apology,' I said, with my usual aplomb, quite myself again. 'I certainly appear to have slipped up on this occasion. Here are three more. You will find nothing wrong with them.'

He examined them, muttering to himself in wop, and cheered up immediately. 'It is very well!' he chortled. 'The matter is finished.'

'I'll take the others, so,' I said casually, putting out my hand. 'I mean to have it out with that bookie!'

But Fate had another little bombshell up her sleeve.

'I am sorry, I must retain them,' he said, as genially as if I were a well-loved friend. 'The police were here, with instructions. There are many of these forgeries going around. I have also to trouble you for your name and address. A pure formality, but those are the police orders.'

My heart sank. I felt as if I should faint. The police! My name and address! A pure formality! But Santorelli was waiting and I dared not falter. Long ago I settled a name and address for this kind of situation, the way it would trip off my tongue like a real one: Thomas Merton, 29 Cumberland Place, NW. But my brain was numb with shock and before I could stop myself I had told him my name was Cruise. Thank God, I still had the presence of mind to give Norah's address, however. If the police came barging in there, she would beat them off as she had beaten off the Social Security bloodhounds. All the same, when at last she emerged from the Ladies, I said nothing of this contretemps, just walked her to a bus stop and myself took a taxi home. No Irish Club for me that afternoon, I needed my wits about me.

It could have been worse, I suppose. If I hadn't had the genuine money with me, Santorelli might have called the police in then and there. But that was the only crumb of comfort in it. At a blow I had lost some three-fifths of my capital, for Bendy's notes were clearly too hot to use again. They would have to be disposed of quickly, what was more, in the river maybe. I still had most of Penny's eight hundred, true, but what had seemed a fortune when I got it now looked like pretty small beer, so easily does the human mind adjust to affluence.

And shortly there would be other huge expenses. Time was moving on and the return of that pestilential Goodge could not be long delayed. Then Brooke would apply to him for an assurance of my respectability and I should be forced to find new lodgings. And pay for them, too. Arabella Road was out, henceforward. My intention had been, after my second windfall, to offer a quarter's rent in cash, because I still, at the time, entertained hopes of marrying Penelope. Even now, after all that happened, they often flicker up. I am the least vain of men, but it seems incredible that charm like mine should leave her wholly untouched. And reviewing her conduct, monstrous as it is, I can't help wondering if I always interpret it correctly. Her refusal of my olive branch after the party, for instance, and her continuing silence now—may she not, woman-like, be simply playing hard-to-get? It strikes me as the probable explanation.

I have looked for signs and portents, and invariably they were in my favour. This same morning, I said a prayer and threw the dice, on the understanding that if two or more aces turned up it would mean that my prospects were bright. And there were three! What could be plainer than that? And now there has come this cruel, crushing blow. I shall have to leave and, in courtship, proximity is half the battle. Out of sight, out of mind, is a hard saying but a very true one. The fires of love need constant stoking if they are not to die, and I'm blest if I know how to do it unless I am there.

*

Really, I am beginning to feel like Job. The morning after the events I have described, at the unearthly hour of a quarter to ten, there was a vigorous pounding on my door as of some one in a violent hurry. I naturally thought it was Penny, turning to me for help in a crisis, and flew to open. It was Norah Kilbane, which put me out of humour right away. Nothing is more vexatious, when you long to see one woman, to find yourself stuck with another, and I have never asked Norah to this house. She does not suit it. If the front door had been properly shut and she had used the intercom I would have told her to wait below till I came; but some fool must have left it ajar.

Before I could reprove her, she burst into a torrent of recrimination, like any old tinker. It seemed the police had called at Arabella Road, at eight o'clock or thereabouts, asking questions by the dozen and all as disagreeable as could be. They had refused to believe I was not on the premises and had insisted on searching the rooms. She had never been so ashamed in her life. It was bad enough, the snoopers and the process-servers, but she drew the line at detectives. And at crime. She was a Christian woman and kept a decent house, and she would not be used as an accommodation address for crooks. On and on and on, you never heard anything like it.

'You didn't tell them where I was?' I slipped in when she finally paused for breath.

'I did not but it was in my mind to,' she stormed. 'And if they come again, I'll likely be forced. You only think of yourself. What about me? Police in the house! The whole road saw them, and their bloody police-car standing a full hour in front of the door!'

She had made this point about the car already more than once, but women like her always repeat themselves over and over.

'The officers had no right to question you,' I told her. 'They have grossly exceeded their duty. You could bring an action.'

'Ah, it's a lawyer you are now, is it? 'Tis yourself I'll be suing before I'm a whole lot older.' Her voice was shrill, like a teased parrot's. 'Just leave me out of your doings, that's all. I won't be dragged in the mud for your convenience.'

'This is all about nothing,' I assured her quietly. 'I kept mum yesterday, for fear you'd be upset. But one of the notes I gave for our lunch was bad, apparently, and Santorelli told me he had to take my name and address on police instructions, as more such notes had been passed in the neighbourhood. It was a pure formality.'

'Was it now? Then why not give your own address? The men were perfectly civil until I said you didn't live there and I didn't know where you were. Then they went on, like they were crazy.'

'Please, Norah, accept my word as a gentleman that I have done no wrong.'

And she wouldn't! She didn't believe that most solemn affirmation and she let me know it. My very first words, she pointed out, were not of regret or apology but of fear that she might have blown the gaff. Innocent men were not afraid. Innocent men gave their real addresses. She dwelt on these trivial points until I was sick and tired of listening to her.

'Will you stop!' I cried at last, in exasperation. 'This isn't like you, Norah. What's got into you at all?'

Her reply to this took my breath away altogether. I was never so surprised in all my life. Indeed, after hearing her, it's doubtful I'll ever be really surprised again. She calmed down of a sudden, bridled, pouted, rolled her eyes at me like a pup and said: 'When are we going to be married, Sean? Everyone's asking me that.'

I could hardly believe my ears. I had a sense of utter betrayal. In the space of a few seconds the creature had laid her true self bare. I had loved and admired her for her womanly kindness and compassion, had put her on a pedestal, prized her as much as my own dear sainted mother—and all that time she was waiting on me, helping me out, feeding me and doing my laundry, she was merely scheming to get herself a husband! It was the kind of horrible shock that turns a man from the sex and drives him, bitter and broken-hearted, into a monastery.

Well, one thing was sure: I'd have to make tracks out of here tomorrow or sooner.

'Why Norah honey, I never knew you felt like that about me,' I said, when I could speak. 'A man without means, of no settled job! How could I ever look after you?'

'I'd do the looking after, the way I always did,' she replied, working the eyes like mad. She had a bit of money and her dress-making, but the way she came out with that, she might be an heiress.

'I could never agree to such an arrangement,' I told her hastily. 'A man needs to hold his head high.'

'You never held it so very high till now,' she observed sharply. 'And it seems to me, living in a place like this and drinking champagne by the bottle, you can't be doing too badly, whether it's the horses or something else.'

God Almighty, the woman was talking like a wife already.

'I got a run of luck all right, but it was only a flash in the pan,' I said. 'Don't get the wrong idea from the lunch, I wanted to share my winnings with you after all your goodness to me. But for a long time, Norah, I have been weary of this life I lead, its sordid expedients, its striving after base material ends. I was never born for it, it does violence to my nature. Seriously, now, I have been considering if I shouldn't go for the priesthood.'

'Well, isn't it the strangest thing?' she snapped. 'Whenever you talk marriage to an Irishman, it turns out he's heading for the clergy.'

So she'd tried it on before! I wasn't even the first.

'I should have thought a happy Christian home and a family would be enough for you and your spiritual nature,' she went on, nasty as could be. 'There is nothing sordid in that.'

Happy Christian home, how are you! Kids everywhere, washing all over the place, measles, ringworm, the smell of cabbage, family outings on Sunday afternoon, especially those. I don't know why, a man walking out with his wife and children always looks a perfect fool.

'We'll not have to be in too great a hurry,' I said, playing for time. 'Marriage is for life, after all. And this is a bolt from the blue, you caring like that. You've made me a happy man, Norah, happy and proud, but I can't get used to it all at once.'

'But you'll think it over?' she persisted.

'I will indeed.'

So that was that. Her waspishness fell away, now she supposed I was in the bag. She sat there, piling endearments on me and prattling about the future, till I thought she would never go. No more was heard about the police and their persecution. Maybe it had all been a ruse, to frighten me into surrender. You can never know, with scheming women, how much to believe of what they say.

At last she went off, after telling me to have sense and not to be drinking. It brought home to me what marriage with her would be like, and spurred me on to plan my escape. My only hope, now, lay in complete and final disappearance : yet where should I go? There's a weird grapevine in the Irish community that never seems to fail. Police, taxmen, may be hunting for us high and low without success, but our fellow-countrymen put the hand on us at the drop of a hat.

I thought and thought until I felt as if my brain were bursting. No sooner did I get an idea than I realised there was some insurmountable objection to it. And then, all at once, when I was on the point of despair, it was as if a quiet gentle voice were speaking to me. It told me, I should not be struggling and contriving on my own account but should refer my problems to higher powers than mine. It is truly sad how this, which ought to be our first recourse, is so often only tried after we have run through all the others. Humbly, then, I commended my troubles to the Mother of Good Counsel and left them in her dear and loving hands; and went off, refreshed in spirit, for a bite of lunch at the Cypriot café and an afternoon in the Irish Club.

Seven

Now really, at last, the clouds are rolling back, the sun breaks through and a new life opens before me. Help has come, from a quarter where I never thought to find it. In a matter of days, of hours almost, I shall be safe from the police, the snoopers and Norah alike. Yesterday, I was in the depths of despair, utterly discouraged, unable to see one glimmer of hope in the way ahead. This morning, I am on top of the world. Already, the events of the past few days seem no more than an evil dream.

My humble faith in the Mother of us all was not deceived. My love for her is requited, beyond my deserving, which makes it only more precious. By the very first post today came a long letter from Bendy. He was in Spain, at a spot called Torremolinos, and riding high. It was Bendy all over, there were no post-mortems, no details as to how he shook off the police or came to leave the country. His tale was all of the present, of Torremolinos, the bars, discos, nightclubs, the pretty girls and rich old women, especially the last.

'Honest to God, I hardly paid for a thing since I landed,' he wrote. 'And certainly not for a meal. Irish charm does a lot for you in London, but here it's fantastic.'

I had to stop and laugh at that, because Bendy has all the charm of warmed-up cabbage. He makes his way through life by the wag of his tongue, and he's a maestro there for sure.

'It's as easy as falling off a log,' he went on. 'You see an old trout, dressed up to the nines, sitting or walking alone and looking wistful. So up you go and say whatever comes into your head, and it works every time. Before you know it, you're off to some restaurant she's heard of, where she wouldn't like to go unescorted. Probably thinks there are white-slavers lurking under the tables. Sometimes one of them wants you to go home with her afterwards, and then I tell her it's against my religion. The English and the Americans mostly lay off at that and think all the better of you, but Scandinavians are shockingly tenacious. I was badly cornered the other day by an old Swede with a face like a bloodhound. We had a slap-up meal at this joint she knew and then she asked where I lived, so she could drop me home. Away with us in her Dodge, all leather and chromium and gadgets, and what does she pull on me, only drive out to her villa along the coast, miles from anywhere! What could I do? There's such a thing as common politeness after all, and it would have been a bloody long walk home. I just had to grit my teeth and go through with it. Fair play for the old bag, she gave me a Parker pen and some jade cufflinks, but it was a gruelling experience all the same. Now when they offer me lifts I say I need exercise.

He made it all sound like fairyland. I had to admire the fellow, taking off for a distant shore where he'd never been, whose language he couldn't speak, and falling on his feet like a cat dropped from a window. Frankly, I would never have had the nerve. It scared me enough coming to London, full though it was with lads from home, ready to show me around and give me advice. But abroad! foreigners! no one to turn to! no Irish clubs! I'd never stand up to an ordeal like that.

'I have what they call a studio flat,' he continued, 'two rooms, kitchen, bath, balconies to sit out in the cool of the evening. Tomar el fresco, they call it here. It's nicely furnished, with everything found, no end of hot water and a girl coming in to clean. The people are very trusting, just gave me the key and never asked for a penny so far. Now listen, Sean, here's what you'll do. Come on out and join me, and we'll have some fine old cracks together. You'll be a wow in a place like this and it's what I feel the want of, a friendly Cork voice, a decent Corkman to talk things over with me. However much you may be enjoying life, it is a bad thing to live among strangers all the time. You could be slipping into foreign ways before you knew where you were, contaminated in spite of yourself. And sure, what is there to keep you in London now? If the money is short with you, haven't I plenty, for God's sake, and amn't I telling you anyhow, we'll hardly need it?'

These manly words warmed the very cockles of my heart. They breathed out a generosity that you only find among our people, although I do remember a missionary telling me once that Africans were much the same. No question here of Bendy, on to a good thing, keeping it all to himself. His first impulse was to share it with a friend and, by the way he put it, to suggest that the friend would confer a favour on him. I am the last man alive to blow the national trumpet or to indulge in nationalist vainglory; but I do believe it may be said with truth, there's no one like the Irish.

Another thing that touched me deeply—for I own to being different in this respect—was, that he made this offer to *me*, that he bore me not the slightest grudge for the past. When he asked me earlier on to join him in his Continental business, saying how much he needed help, I had refused point-blank, and rudely. 'It's crime, what you're doing there,' I said. 'I'll have no part in it.' If anyone had used such talk to me, he would never have been forgiven. And somehow or other, if it was the last thing I did, I would have had to pay him back. Yet, when Bendy saw me in the library, he greeted me as if those cruel words had never been spoken. He had proved himself the better Christian then and there, and now, when he was on the up and up, leading an honest life and flourishing on it, he had added to his stature in this truly noble way.

His next words were typical of him too, full of kindly thought and concern.

'Don't pay the normal air ticket, whatever you do,' he wrote. 'Take one of the package holidays, all-in for hardly more than a single fare itself. Then, once you're here, tell the hotel you ran across a friend and are staying with him, and most of it will be refunded. Save where you can—that's my motto.'

I was to cable the day and hour of my arriving, so that he could meet me at the airport. And he was mine as always, Bendy. Thus, in a cool practical manner, he had solved all my problems and opened the door to a future radiant with promise.

The prospects were so wonderful, I even forgot how scared I was of flying. I rushed out to make the arrangements and send him the wire, just as he told me. It was quickly done, and I got a package deal for the very next evening. That left me with the rest of today and most of tomorrow to fill in somehow. I was in such a fever of anticipation that I hardly knew what to be at. Once I had brought this memoir up to date, there seemed nothing left but to sit and twiddle my thumbs.

And then all of a sudden, I really can't explain it, the fancy took me to call and say goodbye to Penelope. I should be taking leave of her without a twinge of regret, for my new chances had pushed everything else to the back of my mind. That may have been the reason, perhaps, the idea of bidding a calm farewell to one who lately had meant so much, had so occupied my thoughts, caused me such pain, flitted so constantly in and out of my dreams. And there may have been something else as well, because I am only human. Perhaps I was hoping to see a little sign of grief on her part, a sense of loss, now that I was really to go out of her life for good. For I could not, and did not, believe that I meant nothing to her whatsoever. She had looked at me so sweetly, with such admiration, that time I was telling her of the Singhs and their troubles, and my efforts on their behalf. She was comparing my warm Irish humanity with her cool practical common sense, and owning herself my inferior. It was impossible, after that, that she could be wholly indifferent to me now.

The more I pondered, the more likely it seemed that this was true. I decided to pack before I called, as she would probably wish me to spend my last evening in London with

178

her, and tomorrow there would be no time. Everything was carefully mapped out: I would slip quietly away first thing in the morning, leave my luggage at the terminal, dispose of Bendy's notes somehow, go to confession and Holy Communion in case of a crash and then, with everything off my mind, wait in the Club until I went to the airport.

The packing was soon dealt with. I would take nothing with me but my few clothes. The flat, with Norah's things, the easel, paints, smock, the forest of empty bottles, was to be left just as it stood. It was the first time in my life that I ever had a place to myself, that I could call my own, but thanks to Bendy I was leaving without a pang. Bert might come in and help himself to whatever he fancied, and I would never begrudge it. My break with the past was to be absolute and complete.

*

I am continuing this at midnight and will have to write like mad, as it seems I have found a publisher. At least, he wants me to send the manuscript in, and he doesn't care if it isn't typed. Once more, I have the feeling I so often do, that nothing happens by chance, that all is ordained for the best by the Power above. But for that sudden urge to see Penelope again, the events I am about to describe would never have taken place. I would not have met this fellow who was looking out for the very class of material that I can provide. How true it is, that not one sparrow shall fall on the ground without the Father!

I would gladly dwell on this at greater length. Looking over these pages a while ago, the single fault I found was, my spiritual side does not altogether come through. Money, jobs, drink, the petty cares of daily life, loom larger than they ought if I am to put my whole nature across. It must be, the godless environment contaminated me before I knew it, as Bendy warned could happen. But time presses and I will have to hurry on.

179

That the events of the evening were laid out for me by the Lord, I have told you, I truly believe. This does not mean that all were to my liking. One cruel incident threw a shadow over everything else. I will carry the scar of it in my soul to the end of my life. At the memory of it now, my mind starts whirling again with anger, grief and shock, and a kind of numb incredulity that such things could be. O the irony of it! For, from what the publisher said, they are the very ones that will commend my story to him most. How his eyes will sparkle as he reads!

And so to work.

When I knocked on Penelope's door, it was opened by an old girl in a dress too young for her and with a comical hairdo. Yet there was a family something in her face and I said, quick as lightning, 'You'll be Penelope's mother.'

'Aunt,' she said, smiling. 'How clever of you, though! Come in. My niece is out at work, and I am all by myself.'

Out at work, was she? So little Miss Butler occasionally tells a fib, like anyone else, for all her high and mighty airs. As I followed the aunt inside, I wondered what the reason could be for this particular one, and what queer sort of a family this was, when they didn't all know each other's business.

'Would you like some tea?' the aunt was saying.

'Thanks, I'd rather try a little whisky, if it's all the same.'

She burst out laughing at that, as if I'd said something clever, but she poured it out at once, a real good one, Irish size. Not like that blessed niece of hers, with her 'Then you'd better be off to the nearest low pub,' and looking me up and down as if I had been a tinker.

'You must be Irish,' auntie said, still laughing as she handed it to me. 'Drinking at this hour of the day!'

She would have led a sheltered life all right, as it was nearly three o'clock. Be that as it may, from the word go I was a smash hit with her, a real knock-out. It was a case of love at first sight, as I knew from its happening so often before. That sparkle in her eyes, the little blush that came and went . . . I normally speak, as I write, a perfect upper-class English but now I put on a touch of the brogue for her and she was mad for it.

'That's a fine creation you have on you there, ma'am,' I ventured to say, referring to her youthful attire. 'Elegance itself!'

'Oh, do you mean it?' she asked shyly, smoothing her skirt and blushing again. 'Dear me, it's quite a while since anyone noticed what I wore!'

I'll bet. But she was so nice, you wouldn't really want to be laughing at her. It was strange to be there in Penelope's flat, with Penelope's things all round, and to have some one that looked so like her, even if old, behaving to me as she never did. I had vainly tried my luck with the niece and got off with the aunt in one. Life is a chancy business.

Well, we chatted away of this and that, with auntie topping my glass up whenever it got low, as if she knew me well. She was up from the country, 'doing' London, she loved it at this time of year and all that kind of thing. Then I asked at what hour Penelope got back from her 'work' and she told me, about six as a rule, but today they were meeting in town. That was too bad, I said, because I was going abroad tomorrow and I particularly wanted to say goodbye. And she replied at once, like I was one of the family, that I had better come along too. She was a darling woman altogether.

'We're going to a cocktail party at some publishers,' she said. 'I'll ring them up and say I'm bringing a friend. Penny would never forgive me if I let you run away.'

But first, she was going to have some tea and a sandwich, if I'd excuse her. She was unaccustomed to alcohol and thought it best to fortify herself with a snack, in case the cocktails went to her head. With that she bustled off to the kitchen, leaving me to my own devices.

I had no intention of doing anything in her absence except maybe freshen the glass up if she stayed out for long. But as I sat there, looking at those luxurious flowers and ornaments and pictures, it came to me that I was seeing them for the very last time. A chapter of my life was about to close. I had a sense of things perpetually moving on, perpetually cleared away to make room for others, of ourselves borne along on the tide as we travelled towards eternity.

Suddenly I was restless, fidgety, unable to sit quiet in my chair. I wandered about the room, sniffing the roses, picking things up and putting them down, softly opening the drawers of the writing-table, idly scanning the correspondence inside. On top of the desk was a large silver box, and I opened that. There were ten-pound notes in it, five of them, which must have come from the Bank that day, they were so crisp and clean.

And so respectable, so smug, the property of an assured young woman who never would know what it was to fight and scheme and worry. What came over me then I really can't say, but I took out one of Bendy's notes, the last I still carried round, and laid it on top of the others. It seemed only a marvellous joke at the time. I had a vision of little Miss Nose-in-air toppled, caught as I had been but in some Ritzy place where she went for her finery, questioned, flustered, all at sea, her name and address taken like that of a common offender. It would do her a power of good to come off her high horse a while, and there was no real harm in it. Once they started their probing, they'd find nothing to connect her with the Amsterdam crowd. And it was a last little gesture from me before our lives went their different ways for ever.

*

We were late getting off to those cocktails. Auntie dawdled in the kitchen and then came back wheeling a trolley on which there was tea, cucumber sandwiches and cream buns in a silver basket. She had put out cups for two and was disappointed that I didn't join her. 'Tea is the nicest meal of the day, I always think,' she remarked. Maybe it is, I never tried it, or anyhow nothing along those lines. So she munched her way through the lot, with me looking on and making conversation.

'I wonder now, has Penny a job at all,' I said at one point. 'Or has she a boyfriend tucked away, that's keeping her busy? I never heard of her working till this.'

'Of course she has a job if she says so,' auntie replied. 'She always speaks the truth.'

'You sound very sure of that!'

'Well, I am, too,' she said placidly. 'After her parents died, I brought her up.'

That convinced me more than ever that she was an angel. If my own dear mother had a fault, it was never to believe a blessed word I said. Auntie now went on to reveal some more of her holy simplicity. 'My niece would have to have a job, and a well-paid one too, to live in a flat like this, wouldn't she?' she smiled. Honest to God, I felt a better man only to hear her talking.

At last the good soul finished her meal and went away to put on her hat. I was so much under the spell of her, I nearly removed that note from the box and let Penelope off the hook, but she was back before I had made up my mind. Her hat was amazing, for all the world like one of those baskets of flowers the London people hang from their windows, but I saw she was delighted with it and I made her a pretty speech. Then off we went to find a taxi, with the people in the street turning round to look at us, and presently we landed at the Lombardy Rooms in Mayfair, not a stone's throw from the Jesuit Fathers and as swell a joint as you could hope to see.

I was never in anything like it before. The carpets were so thick and soft, you sank into them as you sink in the mossy turf of moorlands at home. A fellow in fancy dress like something out of a play led us towards an open door, through which came a steady buzz, everyone talking and nobody listening. He asked our names and I gave all mine, with the extra two I add on when I want to make an impression; and he rolled them out so grandly, he seemed to be announcing the Duke of somewhere. Then he stood aside to let us pass.

The room was packed with the weirdest-looking people. You

could see that here was the cream of London intellectual life. I felt at home at once and that this was the kind of society to which I belonged myself of natural right. I told them all how happy I was that my engagements had not prevented me coming. In no time they were asking each other who I was, while Auntie looked on with loving pride. One of these days, I thought, a party like this will be given for me, and my heart leaped up in anticipation.

And then I caught sight of Penelope, beautiful as a dream in her lilac dress. She was staring at me in utter consternation. Of course, it would surprise her, me coming along like this, she was not to know that, to all intents and purposes, I was one of the family now. I hurried across to where she stood and, taking advantage of our new connection, gave her a brotherly kiss, explaining in the next breath how things stood between her aunt and me.

I spoke warmly and sincerely, and as if nothing had ever gone badly between us : as if she had never snubbed or slighted me, egged Caroline on, ignored my olive branch afterwards : as if she had never told me, 'go drink in a pub with some of your low companions' : as if she hadn't lost me my job and exposed me to the last extremities of want in this cruel city. All such wrongs, in that moment, were entirely expunged from my mind. But she merely looked at me as if I were dirt and began to walk away.

Shocked, grieved, incredulous, I hurried after her and begged to know what the matter could be. Her only reply was, that she wished to speak to her aunt. I asked what she had in mind to say to that lady, and never to my last hour will I forget the answer she gave.

'Merely,' she said—and this to my face, in tones of envenomed sweetness—'that you are a thief, a fraud and a confidence trickster !'

Reader, you will hardly believe it, but I swear those were her very words. She hadn't even the manners to lower her voice. Only that everyone was bawling at the top of their lungs, the whole room must have heard them. I, an Irish gentleman, descendant of kings, a thief, a fraud, and a trickster! No woman alive shall speak like that to CRUISE. Did she come into her house and find me in the very act of robbing her safe, I yet would not brook the use of such expressions.

I was swept by a fury such as I never experienced before in my life. I felt ready to burst. Now all the wrong she had done me came back to my mind in a flash, yes, and all that her race had done to mine through the long dark centuries. It was of course because she had wronged me that she hated me thus, so vile is human nature.

And what in the name of God did she mean by it? Nothing. She had merely picked those three epithets out at random and hurled them at me in her spite, regardless of truth or justice. All right, there were the eight hundred pounds, but she knew nothing of that. And there was no theft or fraud involved in it either, it was a simple case of her making restitution. If she hadn't lost me my job, I'd have earned that much and over by now. She really ought to pay me some more. And she'd never miss a paltry sum like that, it was a drop in her ocean. But why am I saying all this, when she couldn't even know what had happened?

Oppression has taught us Irish to hide our feelings, however, and patiently to bide our time. Penelope would smart for this, but for the moment I turned it off as a joke. I teased her lightly about the job her aunt believed she was doing, and the next thing was, she called me a blackmailer and a liar too. Let her wait! but I smiled this off as well, with the suave dignity that never deserts me and, turning on my heel, went back to the others.

From then onward I was the life and soul of the party and kept them all in a roar. The rage that seethed within my breast spurred me on to greater and greater brilliance. A little gnome with a foreign accent said he was sure I must be a writer, to have the command of words like that. I replied that it was so, and smart of him to spot it. He asked who published me, and

I said that hitherto I had written for my own amusement merely. Then he inquired what I was working on now, and I told him, an account of the hardships I had undergone as an Irish exile in London.

'Kepital! kepital!' he chirped, his eyes glinting behind his goggles. 'We are doing a series on immigration. Have you experienced racism? discrimination? bureaucratic interference or harassment? Have you done your level best to integrate, only to meet with hostility and suspicion? Have you a sense of being rejected?'

'I certainly have, the whole damn lot,' I said; and I could not keep a tremor out of my voice. 'This lady beside me here is the only one that ever was kind.'

'You poor dear boy,' said Auntie, patting my hand.

After that, nothing would content the publisher until I had promised to let him see the manuscript. By now the party was breaking up. I looked round for that vixen Penelope, but she had gone. A little plan for her was taking shape at the back of my mind. It involved getting into the flat on the following day while she was out on her 'job', but I foresaw no difficulty there. Auntie was in the bag, I could do whatever I liked with her. Why, I invited her next to come on and eat with me and, when they brought the bill, told her without a blush that I had left my wallet at home! And she was tickled pink. 'So *Irish*, so *unworldly*,' she laughed, and paid for it all herself.

So here I am, at midnight, writing these last few lines. There will be no time to polish them, but they come straight from a full and aching heart. What I said to that publisher was perfectly true. I do have a sense of being rejected by London, had it long before Penelope's fiendish thrusts caused my cup to overflow. But I reject London also, in my turn. I despise it utterly, pagan, materialist and hypocritical as it is. There is no room anywhere here for an artist and a dreamer. Tomorrow I shake the dust of it off my feet for good. I gave it every chance, but time and again it failed me. Now let it go its dismal way in my absence.